Wolfpack Leader

James Mullins

Published By: Longinus Publishing

All rights reserved. This book may not be reproduced in any form, in whole or in part, without written permission from the author.

This is a work of fiction. All characters and events portrayed in this book are either products of the author's imagination or used fictitiously.

©2025 James Mullins First Printed Edition published May 30th,

2025

10 9 8 7 6 5 4 3 2 1

ISBN: 9798285045700

PROLOGUE

Spain, July 1937

As Flight Sergeant Veikko Niemi crossed the airfield, dust rose beneath his boots as the rising sun painted the eastern sky crimson. The Italian Legionary Air Force Fiat CR.32 biplanes sat in a neat row. The bi-plane's canvas-covered frames still glistened with dew. Around them, ground crews swarmed like ants, checking cables, tightening struts, and feeding ammunition belts into the Breda machine guns.

Veikko adjusted his leather flight jacket against the morning chill. Despite the Mediterranean climate, dawn carried a bite that reminded him of Finland's autumn mornings. His fingers traced the patch on his shoulder; the winged lion of the Italian Legionary Air Force, not the blue on white roundel of his homeland.

"Niemi! Over here!" Captain Marco Bianchi waved from the briefing tent. A cigarette dangled from his lips, and smoke curled above his slicked-back dark hair.

Veikko quickened his pace. The Italian was a veteran with seventeen confirmed kills. The kind of pilot Finland's High Command wanted him to learn from. That's why they'd encouraged him to volunteer when the civil war erupted in Spain. "You speak Italian fluently," his commander had said. "Go learn how the Soviets fight. Then come back and teach us. We may need that knowledge someday."

Inside the tent, pilots clustered around a table where maps lay weighted with spent shell casings. The squadron commander, Major Raffaele Chiostri, looked up as they entered. His weathered face creased into a frown.

"Gentlemen," Chiostri began without preamble, "Republican bombers hit Nationalist supply depots near Teruel last night. Intelligence reports Soviet SB-2s repositioning for another strike this morning." His finger traced a line across the map. "This is the likely approach vector here, with fighter escort."

Bianchi leaned in, elbows on the table. "How many?"

"Six bombers. Unknown number of I-16s." Chiostri's gaze swept the faces surrounding him. "These aren't Spanish pilots. They're Soviet 'volunteers'. Trained killers sent by Stalin to test their equipment and tactics."

A murmur rippled through the gathered men. They'd all heard stories about the Soviet pilots especially the I-16 squadron led by a man named Chernyavin. "Takeoff in twenty minutes," Chiostri continued. "Standard interception formation. Bianchi, you'll take Niemi as your wingman."

Bianchi nodded, glancing at Veikko with an appraising look. "Stay on my tail, Finn. No heroics."

"Yes, sir," Veikko replied in flawless Italian, earning a few raised eyebrows from newer pilots who hadn't yet heard the foreigner speak.

As the briefing concluded, Bianchi pulled Veikko aside. "First combat mission?" he asked, lighting a fresh cigarette.

"Yes, sir."

"Forget everything you learned in training. Up there—" he jabbed his cigarette toward the sky, "—it's chaos. Don't think, react, and whatever happens, do not separate from your wingman."

"Understood."

Bianchi studied him for a moment. "The Soviets have a hunter among them. Flies an I-16 with a red star painted larger than regulation on the fuselage. If you see him, break away immediately. That's Chernyavin."

Veikko frowned. "I've heard the name whispered amongst the other pilots."

"He's their best and a ruthless killer. Rumor says he was their top aerobatics instructor before being sent here." Bianchi crushed his cigarette under his boot. "He doesn't fly like the others. He doesn't attack; he executes."

The Fiat growled beneath Veikko as he taxied into position, the vibration traveling up through the stick into his bones. Ahead, Bianchi's aircraft began rolling, gathering speed until its wheels lifted from the dusty strip. Veikko pushed his throttle forward and felt the familiar surge as the biplane accelerated.

The ground fell away, and suddenly the vista of eastern Spain spread before him. He saw large mountains purple with distance, valleys lush with summer crops, villages clustered like pale scabs on the landscape. Below them, Nationalist troops appeared as specks moving along roads, the flash of their vehicles catching morning sunlight.

Veikko slid into formation on Bianchi's right wing, just far enough back to avoid his slipstream. Eight other CR.32s formed up around them, engines droning in unified determination. Through his goggles, Veikko scanned the horizon, his heart pounding against his ribs. Not fear exactly. Perhaps anticipation mixed with a thimble full of fear.

His headset crackled. "Maintain radio discipline," came Chiostri's voice. "Enemy reported ten kilometers northeast, heading southwest at two thousand meters."

For fifteen minutes, they flew in silence, climbing to position themselves above the expected Soviet route. Then Bianchi's arm extended, pointing. "There. Contacts at eleven o'clock."

Veikko squinted against the glare. Dark shapes materialized against the blue canvas of sky, twin-engine bombers flying in tight formation, their silhouettes stark and predatory. Around them, smaller specks orbited like angry wasps. *The I-16s.*

Chiostri's voice cut through the static: "Engage the fighters first. Clear the path to the bombers."

Bianchi banked toward the approaching formation, and Veikko followed, staying tight on his leader's wing. His mouth went dry as the distance closed rapidly. The enemy fighters spotted them, breaking their protective pattern to rise and meet the interceptors.

Everything happened at once. The neat formations dissolved into swirling chaos as aircraft twisted, climbed, and dove in a lethal ballet. Tracers crisscrossed the sky like luminous threads weaving a tapestry of death.

"Follow me in!" Bianchi shouted, diving toward an I-16 that had separated from its companions.

Veikko rolled in behind him, adrenaline flooding his system. The Soviet pilot saw them coming and broke hard left, but Bianchi anticipated the move, cutting inside the turn. Veikko struggled to maintain position as G-forces slammed him against his seat.

Bianchi's guns stuttered, orange flashes at his wingtips. The I-16 jerked, smoke streaming from its engine cowling. It rolled inverted and dived, trailing black smoke as it plummeted toward the earth.

"One down!" Bianchi called. "Stay with me—"

But his words were cut short as two more I-16s slashed through their formation from above. Veikko instinctively yanked the stick, rolling away from the attack. Tracers whizzed past his cockpit, close enough that he felt the displacement of air.

In the chaos, he lost sight of Bianchi. His heart lurched as he realized he was alone, separated from the protection of his leader. He pulled into a climbing turn, desperately searching for the familiar silhouette of Bianchi's CR.32.

Instead, he found himself face to face with an I-16, the aircraft distinctive not just for its stubby, barrel-like fuselage, but for the oversized red star emblazoned on its side. The pilot's goggles caught the sunlight as their gazes locked across the empty space. *Chernyavin.*

Veikko's throat constricted. The Soviet ace was already

rolling toward him, positioning for a firing pass. With a surge of panic, Veikko shoved the stick forward, diving to gain speed. The Fiat responded sluggishly compared to the nimble I-16.

He pulled into a tight turn, trying to shake his pursuer, but Chernyavin stayed with him, matching every move with uncanny precision. Veikko had never seen anyone fly with such controlled aggression. It wasn't just skill; it was artistry.

Tracers flashed past Veikko's wingtip. He jinked right, then left, heart hammering. A glance over his shoulder showed the I-16 still there, closing the distance.

In desperation, Veikko attempted a maneuver he'd practiced but never used in combat a tight Immelmann turn that would reverse his direction while gaining altitude. He pulled the stick back hard, climbing vertically, then rolling inverted at the top of the arc.

For a moment, it seemed to work. The I-16 overshot his position. Veikko's spirits soared as he rolled upright, preparing to dive on his opponent's tail.

Unfortunately, the wily veteran flyer had anticipated the move. Instead of pursuing, he'd executed a climbing barrel roll that positioned him perfectly as Veikko completed his maneuver. The Soviet was already firing as Veikko realized his mistake.

Bullets ripped through the Fiat's fuselage like a giant's fingers tearing tissue paper. One round punched through the instrument panel, sending glass fragments slicing across Veikko's cheek. Another shattered the oil pressure gauge, spraying hot fluid into the cockpit.

The engine coughed, sputtered, then began to smoke. Warning lights flashed across the panel. The stick grew heavy in Veikko's hands as hydraulic pressure failed. *I'm going down.*

Veikko fought the dying aircraft, wrestling with controls that responded more sluggishly with each passing second. The horizon tilted crazily as the Fiat entered a flat spin, the centrifugal force pushing him deep into his seat.

Through the smoke filling his cockpit, he glimpsed Chernyavin's I-16 circling above, watching him fall. Not pursuing for the kill, nor celebrating, just observing with clinical detachment. The act of a hunter noting how his prey dies.

The ground rushed up at terrifying speed. Veikko pulled back on the stick with all his strength, trying to level the wings for a crash landing. The Fiat shuddered, reluctantly responding to his desperate commands.

Impact came with a bone-jarring crash. The right wing struck first, shearing off completely as the aircraft cartwheeled across a fallow field. Metal screamed against earth. The world dissolved into a kaleidoscope of spinning sky and ground.

Then, stillness. The sudden silence roared in Veikko's ears louder than the engine had ever been. He hung suspended in his harness, blood trickling from his forehead into his right eye. Every breath sent daggers of pain through his chest. *Probably broken ribs.* He realized.

In addition to his other injuries, his left arm hung at an odd angle, clearly broken. Smoke poured from the engine cowling. Fire would follow soon. With his good hand, Veikko fumbled with the harness release. The buckle gave way, dropping him hard against the cockpit side.

Pain erupted through his body, nearly blacking him out. He forced himself to stay conscious, clawing his way out of the shattered cockpit. His boots touched soil, and his legs crumpled beneath him. He dragged himself away from the wreckage, leaving a trail through the dirt like a wounded animal.

A familiar engine sound made him look up. The I-16 was making a low pass over the crash site. Chernyavin's aircraft was so close that Veikko could see the pilot's face as he looked down at the wreckage. Their eyes met again through the windscreen, dark, calculating eyes set in a face removed from emotion.

The Soviet pilot tilted his wings slightly, not a salute, but an acknowledgment, before banking away toward the east, climbing back to rejoin the combat still raging above.

Veikko collapsed onto his back, the Spanish sun beating down on his face. In the distance, he heard vehicles approaching, Nationalist troops coming to recover him, if they reached him before the Republicans.

He stared at the sky where Chernyavin had disappeared, committing every detail of the encounter to memory. The precise movements and ruthless efficiency. The way he'd anticipated every defensive maneuver he tried to make.

I'll remember, Veikko thought through the haze of pain, *and next time, I'll be ready for you.*

The hospital in Salamanca smelled of antiseptic and blood. Veikko stared at the ceiling, counting cracks in the plaster to distract himself from the throbbing in his newly set arm. Two weeks since being shot down, and the humiliation still burned hotter than his injuries.

A knock at the door drew his attention. Captain

Bianchi entered, his left arm bandaged, but otherwise intact. He carried a bottle of wine and two tin cups.

"You look like hell, Finn," he said, pulling up a chair.

"You should see the other guy," Veikko replied dryly.

Bianchi snorted, pouring wine into both cups. "The other guy is still flying." He handed a cup to Veikko. "Chernyavin got another one yesterday. That makes twenty-six confirmed kills."

Veikko took the wine with his good hand. "You saw it happen?"

"From a distance. Same pattern as with you. He isolates his target, forces them to make a defensive move, then counters before they've completed their maneuver." Bianchi sipped his wine. "It's like he can read their minds, or maybe he just knows what a desperate pilot will try."

Veikko stared into his cup. "He doesn't fight like the others."

"No. The rest of them fly like soldiers. He flies like..."

"Like a wolf," Veikko finished. "Patient. Calculating. Always three moves ahead."

Bianchi nodded. "The Nationalists are calling his group 'The Wolfpack' now."

They sat in silence for a moment, the sounds of the busy hospital filtering through the thin door.

"What will you do now?" Bianchi finally asked. "Return to Finland?"

Veikko shook his head. "Not yet. I'm staying until I figure out how to beat him."

"It might not be you who does."

"Maybe not," Veikko admitted. "But someday, someone will. And I want to know how." He looked Bianchi in the eye. "We might need that knowledge in Finland sooner than you think."

Bianchi nodded slowly, understanding in his eyes. Everyone knew Stalin's ambitions wouldn't stop at Spain. "Then study him," he said. "Learn from this defeat."

"I intend to." Veikko raised his cup in a toast. "To lessons written in blood."

"And to surviving them," Bianchi added, clinking his cup against Veikko's.

That night, as nurses moved quietly through darkened corridors, Veikko lay awake, replaying every second of his encounter with Chernyavin. He dissected each maneuver, each decision, searching for the pattern that might someday reveal a weakness. *What must I do to kill the wolf?*

Chapter 1

November 30, 1939

Forward Finnish Airfield, near Viipuri

The sky cracked open over Viipuri. A low moan sounded first, like wind through dead timber, but it rose into a shriek. Next came thunder, and then the unmistakable percussion of bombs falling in staggered strings across the rooftops of Finland's southern jewel.

Senior Lieutenant Veikko Niemi stood motionless on the hard-packed snow of the dispersal line. Wisps of his breath drifted from his lips as he watched plumes of black smoke twist upward over the city. They reached toward the brittle late November sky like grasping fingers.

"Viipuri's burning," Flight Sergeant Paavo Lehto muttered behind him.

"I can't believe they've actually done it," Veikko replied.

Seeking reassurance, Lehto asked, "The Soviet Union

is vastly larger than us. Can Finland survive this?"

"I don't know. What I do know is that I will fight to my last breath to drive the invader from our skies."

Lehto slowly nodded agreement. "As will I."

The engines of the four Fokker D.XXIs were already ticking over. The four planes were lined up like blunt-nosed dogs in the dawn light. Vapor hissed from the exhaust stacks. A crewman ran by, cursing the cold as he pulled the ignition trolley away from Paavo's aircraft. Another kneeled under Veikko's wing, thumping the hard rubber of the landing gear.

Across the airfield, klaxons wailed. Somewhere behind the hangars, someone was already shouting for extra fuel drums. Ammunition crates appeared like conjured ghosts. There was no declaration of war. The Russians had skipped the formalities and went right to the killing.

"Mount up!" Veikko snapped. His voice didn't need to carry. They were already moving.

Veikko clambered up the frost-bitten ladder into his cockpit, careful not to let his gloves stick to the icy rail. The metal was biting cold even through layers of wool and leather. He strapped in with fingers that already stung, reached for the primer pump, and gave it three firm squeezes.

The Fokker was primitive compared to the newer planes of the mighty Red Air Force. The plane consisted of fabric and wood over a steel frame. In addition, it was among the final open cockpit monoplanes to enter service. A fact that made the plane very uncomfortable to fly during a Finnish winter. The D.XXI was nimble, and it was all they had to face off against the largest air force in the world.

The crew chief gave him a thumbs-up. Veikko tapped the throttle. The engine coughed, caught, and roared to life with a burst of flame from the exhaust. He taxied to the line, his heartbeat steadily, and his jaw clenched. Over his shoulder, the others followed, Paavo, Corporal Arttu Koskinen, and Second Lieutenant Vesa Haarla. Four pilots. Four D.XXIs. Against what?

He didn't know. The city was a smudge now, a red-stained bruise on the winter horizon. Smoke stacked above it like a funeral pyre. He felt it in his bones. *Viipuri wasn't a target. It was a message. Give up now or we will destroy you.*

Veikko rolled onto the runway, such as it was, packed snow atop frozen earth. Primitive by the standards of Europe's modern air forces. He pushed the throttle forward. The engine responded with a low snarl, then a rising wail as he bounced along the uneven strip. The tail lifted. Then the wings bit air.

He climbed fast and shallow. No clouds or cover. Just naked sky and the weight of the war pressing down on his shoulders. *This is it,* he thought. *This is the beginning.*

Thanks to a couple of semesters spent abroad, he was fluent in Italian. Therefore, the high command encouraged him to volunteer and fly with the Legionary Airforce when the Spanish Civil War erupted. There, he gained invaluable experience against the best the Soviet Union had to offer and the scars to prove it.

The memory of smoke pouring from his Fiat CR.32's engine cowling as he crashed into that Spanish field still visited him in dreams. So did the cold, calculating eyes of the Soviet ace who'd put him there, Major Grigori Chernyavin. Two years had passed since that day, but Veikko's shoulder still ached in cold weather where it had broken in the impact.

The physical pain had faded, but the humiliation of watching Chernyavin's I-16 circle his wreckage like a vulture remained razor sharp. Someday, he'd promised himself during those long weeks in the Salamanca hospital, they would meet again and next time, the outcome would be different.

Veikko pulled back on the stick, his Fokker D.XXI climbing hard into the pale morning sky. Frost-laced canopies glittered in the low winter sun, each breath becoming a silver ghost within his mask. The aircraft shuddered as it passed through a shallow pocket of turbulence.

The engine growled under the strain, but Veikko didn't ease up. He kept climbing, 1,400 meters, then 1,600. His gloved hand was tight on the throttle.

Behind and below, the rest of the flight rose to meet him. Four aircraft, archaic by foreign standards, but Finland had to make use of every airplane they had. Even by doing that the enemy still outnumbered them by thirty to one in the sky.

The air grew thinner, colder, cleaner. His altimeter touched 2,000 meters. He leveled off. Viipuri burned beneath them.

The city unfolded below him like a siege painting come to life. Viipuri. His childhood home and the first school he attended was somewhere beneath that haze. The corner bookstore his mother used to take him to, long gone now in the roiling columns of smoke.

Flames leaped from shattered rooftops and apartment blocks. Black plumes curled skyward, marking the impact sites of high explosive bombs dropped from the Soviet SB-2 bombers. Near the market square, a second detonation lit the horizon, a great orange blossom climbing above the stonework and timber. The flames were as bright as a funeral pyre.

"Dear God," Second Lieutenant Vesa Haarla whispered over the radio. "They hit the rail yard."

"Focus," Veikko snapped. His voice cut through the static with a snap of command. "Visual scan. Call what you see."

To his left, Sergeant Paavo Lehto peeled wide. "Contact, north by northeast. Six... no, seven aircraft. SB-2s. Level altitude. No fighter escort spotted."

"They'll have one," Veikko said. "They didn't send bombers this far solo. Eyes sharp."

The Soviet bombers a flew tight and disciplined formation. Their dark green fuselages glinted dully in the winter sun. They resembled blades drawn from shadow, the blood-red stars on their wings and tails glaring down over the burning city like the mark of executioners. Each one looked like a knife poised above the snow-covered city.

Even from this height, Veikko could see motion on the ground, tiny black specks fleeing between buildings. *Civilians.* Smoke curled around them like hands, trying to drag them down. *Viipuri wasn't a target. It was a punishment for daring to defy the will of Stalin.*

"Should we engage now?" Haarla's voice cracked in his headset.

"Negative," Veikko said. "Hold altitude. We get above them first. Then we come down like hammers."

To their rear, Flight Sergeant Arttu Koskinen added, "I

see them. And I've got butterflies the size of crows."

"You'll live, Arttu," Paavo said, dry as frozen earth. "Assuming you shoot straight."

Veikko adjusted the trim on his plane. His eyes fixed on the shapes ahead. Now the dorsal gunners of the SB-2 medium bombers were visible. The Finns could see their bundled silhouettes in the bomber's glass turrets. The gunners appeared to be completely oblivious to the approaching Finns. *Must be concentrating on their handy work below.*

His breath fogged again against the edge of his goggles. He blinked it away. His eyes fell to his gauges and quickly took in everything. *Looks good.*

"Split in pairs," he ordered. "Haarla, you're with me. Paavo, take Arttu. We go in hard and fast. No showboating. Fire and climb."

"Copy that," came the replies.

Veikko rolled into position, thumb resting on the trigger. *Give them cold steel, not fire. Just as my ancestors before me. It's the Finnish way. Fast, efficient, and merciless. Let the Soviets revel in spectacle. I've a city to defend.*

"Engage," he said as he tipped the nose of his plane down.

Veikko's instincts prickled. Below the bomber formation, he caught a flash of motion. Then he saw it, a stubby silhouette, darker than the rest, slipping out from the bomber's shadow line.

"There," Veikko said sharply into his mic. "Escort. I-16, low six o'clock. Climbing."

"Confirmed," Paavo said. "Just one?"

"For now. I'm sure there are more. It would be the height of arrogance to send only one fighter escort with these bombers." Veikko pulled hard on the stick. "I'll take him."

The Fokker's frame groaned under the strain as Veikko banked up and to the left, with his throttle jammed forward. The climb was steep and short. His engine roared as the aircraft surged upward in a tight spiral. The I-16 was faster, but it had bled speed pulling into position behind the bombers. It hadn't seen him yet.

Veikko leveled just above the enemy fighter's altitude and rolled inverted, flipping the nose straight into a dive. The sky tilted, the horizon vanished. The I-16 quickly filled his windscreen, a squat, snub-nosed predator, its canopy glinting as the Soviet pilot twisted his head too late.

Veikko fired. The four synchronized 7.92mm Brownings shuddered in their mounts. Tracers ripped through the sky, carving lines of light into the cold blue morning. Rounds first hit the tail and then the rear canopy of the I-16's fuselage. The glass exploded in a mist of sparkling fragments.

Smoke trailed from its shredded wing root as the enemy fighter dipped hard, nose-down. Veikko held his fire. *No need to waste rounds. The kill was certain.*

"Scratch one," he said into the mic, breathing through clenched teeth as he pulled up and away.

The I-16 spiraled as it fell, trailing a lazy corkscrew of black smoke before vanishing into the tree line southeast of the city. No chute or flares. Just silence where a man had once flown.

Haarla's voice crackled in over the radio. "Clean shot. That was beautiful, sir."

"No such thing," Veikko replied. "Back on me. We hit the bombers next. They've had their turn."

The bombers loomed ahead, wide-bodied and patient, lumbering through the thin blue above Viipuri like beasts unbothered by the chaos they'd left behind. Plumes of black smoke still climbed from the city beneath them, the fires feeding on childhood streets and old stone churches Veikko had once walked past in peace.

Now, he was a hammer. "Pairs. On me," Veikko called over the radio. "Pick a target and break low after your pass. Don't get caught by their gunners."

He rolled the Fokker into position, nose toward the lead bomber. The airframe trembled as he dove. His throttle was pushed forward. The Fokker's speed built fast, as the control surfaces stiffened with the rush of air over them.

Cold wind screamed around the cockpit. Frost flaked from his goggles as he squinted through the shaking sight. The SB-2 filled his view. The plane had wide wings and a glass nose. Its twin engines hummed as if they weren't thirty seconds from hell.

The dorsal turret swung toward him, as the gunner twisted in his seat. It was too late. Veikko pressed the trigger.

The Brownings hammered in rhythm. Tracers sliced through the sky, walked across the left engine cowling, then stitched their way toward the cockpit. He saw the gunner's head snap back, then slump forward. A second later, the fuel lines burst. The engine caught fire with a bright whoosh.

The bomber rolled shallowly, wobbling, then dipped toward the earth trailing flame like a comet. Veikko pulled hard to the right, climbing through the debris field.

"Target down," he called.

"Another smoking!" Paavo barked. "Arttu got one!"

Haarla's voice was tight. "Coming in on the wing of the rear bomber. Gunners active."

Veikko leveled just long enough to see Haarla's Fokker streak past a bomber's flank. Tracers chased him. Two more followed, then a burst of red from the bomber's belly turret.

"Break! Break!" Veikko snapped.

Haarla rolled, hit throttle, and escaped through the gunner's arc. His plane trailed a thin wisp of smoke from a wingtip. "I'm hit but its light. Controls are good."

"Form up. Regroup. No repeats." Veikko banked above the formation, assessing damage. Two bombers were falling away. One was gone. The others were already beginning their turn. "They're running."

"Cowards," Arttu spat.

"No, survivors," Veikko corrected, voice flat, "and we let them live too long."

Below, Viipuri still burned. To Veikko's left, Arttu and Vesa dove in tandem. Arttu's Fokker cut in first, a shallow dive from Veikko's high port side.

His burst raked the belly of the bomber second from the end. Glass shattered. The bombardier folded backward in his harness before the second engine caught, a ripple of flame punching out from the cowling like a furnace door kicked open.

The bomber dipped hard to starboard, as smoke trailed the plane in thick bands. Vesa came in behind him with perfect timing. His shots punched into the wing root of the bomber next in line. The Soviet aircraft banked violently, trying to evade, but Vesa stayed on it for three full seconds.

His bullets chewed through metal and fabric before he peeled away. The bomber's left wing crumpled. The aircraft spiraled once, twice, and broke apart mid-air.

"Two down!" Vesa shouted over the radio, voice trembling with the rush. "Two down and I'm clear!"

"Nice shooting," Veikko said. "Watch your six."

The formation broke. Soviet gunners fired in panic, their bursts wild and erratic as the remaining four SB-2s turned west in staggered retreat. The line they'd held before the attack which had been tight, measured, and confident had fractured into a disjointed pack.

Then Veikko saw Paavo's Fokker punch through a hail of tracers, just above the bomber group. The dorsal gunner on the lead aircraft swiveled fast. Rounds tore across Paavo's fuselage, then the enemy fire stitched a clean line across the right wing. One struck the Fokker's cowling. The engine belched smoke.

"Paavo?" Veikko barked.

"I'm hit." The sergeant's voice came tight with pain. "Throttle's sluggish. Control's still there. I'm heading home."

"Understood. Stay low. Vesa, escort him. Arttu, with

me. We'll ride them out."

Veikko climbed high to watch the remains of the Soviet formation disappear into the haze over Lake Ladoga. They were limping home. The enemy fled, but fear was a short-lived ally.

He took a long, silent breath. The sweat on his back had gone cold. The fires below hadn't dimmed.

Forward Airfield, Outside Viipuri

The wind cut across the field like a razor. Snow blew low to the ground in fine, stinging sheets. Mechanics waited along the edge of the runway, hats pulled low, scarves frozen stiff around their jaws.

The first shape appeared through the haze, a Fokker. The plane limped in low. The engine coughed as smoke trailed from its cowling like a dying breath.

Sergeant Paavo Lehto brought the aircraft in fast, too fast, but he held it steady. One wheel touched, then the other then the whole frame bounced once before settling into a rough roll. The engine sputtered and died just shy of the dispersal line.

Two crewmen ran toward the plane as Sergeant Paavo Lehto slumped sideways over the cockpit's edge with a grunt. His face was pale beneath the rim of his flight helmet and drawn tight with pain. He pressed his left glove hard against his thigh, soaking it in blood in an attempt to slow the bleeding through his flight suit.

"Medic! "one of the crew shouted. The other grabbed Paavo's arm as he tried to swing a leg over the side. "Don't be stupid," the crewman said.

"Too late," Paavo muttered, collapsing into their grasp.

They lowered him down together. The crewmen half-carried and half-dragged him to the med tent while the base's doctor scrambled across the snow. Blood dripped steadily onto the ground. Each of the drops blooming crimson against the white.

Veikko's Fokker came in moments later, wheels skidding along the hard-packed snow. Arttu and Vesa followed, both machines rattling but intact. The airfield crew converged, already shouting to one another as they swarmed the grounded Fokkers.

Men in oil-streaked coveralls dragged ammunition crates through the snow, cracking them open with crowbars and tossing fresh belts to gunners. A pair of mechanics climbed onto Paavo's wing, pried open an access panel, and began probing the engine with gloved fingers numb from the cold.

Fuel hoses hissed. Gun barrels clacked as covers were pulled off and belts fed in. Engines were checked with frozen tools, mechanics cursing through clenched teeth as they worked at speed, fingers too stiff to feel what they were fixing. There was no waiting or pause in their work. The next flight could come in an hour or less.

Someone patted Vesa on the shoulder as he climbed down from his Fokker. Arttu laughed once sharp, and high. He shook his head and used his hands to relive his pass on the bomber. Ground crew crowded around the returning pilots with a mix of awe and fear, as if they were specters who might vanish again with the next scramble.

The base buzzed with tension, and the high of survival. Lieutenant Veikko Niemi said nothing. He walked the line in silence, his flight helmet tucked under one arm, boots crunching in the snow. He didn't speak to Arttu or Vesa. He didn't glance toward the med tent where Paavo had vanished. He didn't celebrate. The men he had killed today weighed on his soul.

He stared up at the pale blue sky and waited for the next enemy to come screaming out of it. Because they would, and next time they might not leave any of them alive. The silence above wasn't peace, it was only the space between strikes.

The voice of Sergeant Mikkola, his crew chief could be heard shouting orders at the fuel team. The team hauled a fuel hose from a half-buried drum, snow crusted on the nozzle and began topping off tanks. Every minute counted. Another alert could come at any second. There was no time to breathe, only reload, refuel, and return to the sky.

There was no celebration. No cheering. Just the hiss of cooling engines, the metallic clatter of toolboxes opening, and the distant smoke from Viipuri as the town burned.

Chapter 2

Forward Airfield, Outside Viipuri

November 30, 1939

The canvas flap slapped once in the wind as Lieutenant Veikko Niemi ducked inside the command tent. A wave of warm air and stale cigarette smoke met him. The faint warmth coming from the wood burning stove was barely enough to thaw the stiffness in his fingers.

Captain Tauno Nieminen looked up from a battered map table. Upon seeing Veikko, his brow furrowed and he clinched his pipe with his teeth. A single kerosene lantern swayed above. The dim light threw shadows across the tent walls and illuminated the faces of two junior officers bent over a list of sortie schedules.

"You're late," Nieminen said without looking at him.

"I was waiting to see if Sergeant Lehto would walk out of the med tent under his own power," Veikko replied. He dropped his flight helmet on the table with a dull thud.

Nieminen grunted, not without sympathy. "Report."

"Four SB-2s escaped. Three confirmed down. One unconfirmed. We destroyed part of the formation before they struck their second target. The city's still burning."

"And you?"

"Intact. Minor damage to Haarla's aircraft. Paavo's hit. Bad, but not fatal."

Nieminen nodded once, then tapped ash from his pipe into an empty tin. "Not bad for our first day."

Veikko didn't answer. He wasn't interested in grading on curves. Flying in Spain taught him how much mercy to expect from the Soviets.

The captain moved to the radio table, manned by Corporal Heiskanen. The young corporal sat hunched, with a set of headphones pressed tight to his ears. A pencil twitched in his right hand like it had a mind of its own. A nervous habit.

"Anything going on?" Nieminen asked.

Heiskanen gave a small nod. "Channel Four. Blue flight, six aircraft on patrol near Antrea. They've spotted something."

"Let's hear it."

Heiskanen flicked the switch, and static filled the tent, jagged and raw. Then a voice cut through. It sounded distant and edged with panic.

"—repeat, four unidentified fighters approaching from the east, high altitude, tight formation—"

Veikko's eyes narrowed. "They're diving now—two from above, two flanking, God, they're moving in sync—

Mikko, break left! Break left!—"

A burst of gunfire crackled through the speaker. "He's hit. T-t-hey clipped him clean, didn't even—"

More static. A different voice. Calmer, but cold. "All positions, this is Blue Four. We are under coordinated attack. Enemy fighters flying in a three-point wedge. Repeat—coordinated attack, tight maneuver discipline. They're not amateurs—"

The line went dead. The tent fell silent. Captain Nieminen slowly straightened. "That wasn't luck."

Veikko stepped closer to the table. "That was rehearsed. Tight turns. Coordinated strike angles. They weren't improvising."

Heiskanen spoke softly, not turning around. "It sounded like they were performing."

Veikko said nothing, but something cold settled into his gut. The radio description had triggered a flash of memory, his Fiat CR.32 spiraling toward Spanish soil, control surfaces shredded by precise bursts that seemed to anticipate his every move. He could still feel his helplessness as enemy fire systematically dismantled his aircraft over Valencia. The Soviet pilot had flown not with the random aggression of most Russian flyers, but with the elegant, deadly precision of a matador. The same signature style he'd just heard described over the radio.

"It can't be," he muttered, almost to himself. Captain Nieminen glanced at him with a raised eyebrow.

"What?" Nieminen asked.

Veikko shook his head. "Nothing. Just... I've seen this before. In Spain. The way they coordinated, coming from multiple angles simultaneously, it's textbook Chernyavin."

"The Red Star commander?" Nieminen's voice was skeptical. "I thought they executed him during Stalin's purges."

"Everyone did," Veikko replied, unconsciously rubbing his left shoulder where it had been broken in the crash. "But if he's alive and flying here, we're in for a harder fight than anyone imagined."

Veikko left the command tent without a word. The wind outside slapped his face like a reprimand. Snow danced low across the packed ground, whispering through boots and under flaps. The distant fires of Viipuri still lit the southern horizon, glowing orange behind the tree line like the afterimage of a bad dream.

A blue cross, hastily painted on canvas, marked the med tent. A pair of stretchers leaned against the entry. One was dusted with snow. The other bore blood that hadn't been cleaned off.

Veikko ducked through the flap. Inside, the air was thick with sweat, iodine, and kerosene. The stove in the corner hissed and popped, radiating enough heat to make the canvas sweat where it sagged low. The light was yellow and dim, barely cutting through the haze. Five cots lined the left wall, two of them occupied. A third man lay on the floor on a bedroll, snoring through a bandaged jaw.

Sergeant Paavo Lehto was propped against a stack of blankets, pale and stiff-jawed. His flight suit had been cut open at the thigh, and a wide dressing was taped tightly across the wound. Blood had soaked through the bandage in a dark, spreading oval. His helmet was gone. His hair was matted to his forehead with sweat.

A medic noticed the saturated bandage and decided it

was time to change it. He removed the blood-soaked dressing and tightened a fresh bandage on the leg. He worked with a kind of numb efficiency that came from long practice.

Paavo looked up and smirked.

"Still alive, sir."

Veikko pulled up a stool and sat without a word. He took a long look at the wound, then at Paavo's face. The pilot looked ten years older than he had three hours ago. His skin was pale and sweat glistened on his forehead.

"Doc says the bullet missed the femur," Paavo added. "Lucky me."

Veikko nodded once. "How long until you're flying again?"

Paavo chuckled, then winced. "He says a few weeks. I say five days, give or take."

"You won't be flying in five days."

Paavo's smirk widened. "You planning to stop me, sir?"

Veikko didn't answer. The medic finished his work, gave a silent nod, and moved on to the next man. The tent was quiet again, save for the wind outside and the slow hiss of the stove.

Paavo turned serious. "We got two of them, didn't we? Bombers, I mean."

"Three. Maybe four."

"Then it was worth it."

Veikko stood. He looked down at the blood-streaked

floorboards, then back at the sergeant. "Rest while you can."

Paavo replied, "You should too, sir," but Veikko was already gone.

Chapter 3

Forward Airfield, Outside Viipuri

November 30, 1939

The pilot's quarters were a long canvas tent sagging under a crust of snow. Its walls rippled with each gust of wind. Smoke leaked from a bent stove pipe near the center and curled sluggishly into the pale sky.

Inside, the air was thick with smoke, the smell of wool, and the sharp tang of wet canvas. A squat iron stove sat in the middle, its fire low and sullen, casting more shadows than light. Second Lieutenant Vesa Haarla sat on an overturned crate, hunched forward, his gloves still on. Across from him, Corporal Arttu Koskinen crouched by the stove with his arms resting on his knees, eyes lost in the coals.

Neither of them spoke. Veikko stepped in and closed the door behind him. The thud of it made both men flinch.

Vesa looked up first. His face was pale, pinched by wind and strain. "Sir."

Arttu gave a nod but didn't speak. Veikko stepped between the crates and duffels scattered near the stove and crouched beside it, his gloved hands resting on his knees. The heat barely reached past the iron shell, but it bled slowly through his jacket and into his spine. For a moment, the three of them sat close, ringed in dim light and canvas, alive and unsure what to say about it.

Arttu finally broke the silence. "You think Paavo will be back?"

"He's stubborn," Veikko said.

"Yeah," Arttu muttered. "That's not an answer."

Veikko sighed, then slowly nodded. "Yes the doctor told him two weeks, he is aiming for five days. I remember the fire in my chest. Eagerly waiting for my chance to take on the enemy in Spain. I watched too many of my squad mates die and killed too many men to take joy in the deaths of our enemies. They are simply targets that need to be destroyed. Nothing more.

Vesa changed the subject before Veikko's dour mood spoiled the elation from victory the other pilots shared. He rubbed his gloved hands together without taking them off. "We were lucky today."

"No," Veikko said. "The ones who got away were lucky."

Vesa didn't argue. The kettle whistled once, then gave up. The firewood snapped with a sharp pop, and Arttu jumped slightly.

"I froze up for a second," he said, eyes still on the coals. "Lined up my shot on the second pass and just… couldn't pull the trigger. Took me too long. If they'd had a tail gunner with a steadier aim…"

Veikko didn't scold or correct him. He just waited for Arttu to continue.

Arttu continued, "I kept thinking about the guy in that glass bubble. Wondering if he knew he was about to die. If he saw me before the rounds hit him."

"He did," Vesa said. "I saw his head turn."

Arttu reached into his flight coat and pulled out a dented tin cup. He poured a few fingers of black tea from the kettle. His hands trembled just enough for the liquid to slosh.

Veikko put a reassuring hand on Arttu's shoulder. "I know from experience that we'll live in the heads of those pilots that survived. They'll soon spread the word to their comrades. That will make them anxious and anxious men make mistakes."

A smile tugged at the edge of Arttu's lips. "How do you know?"

"Because I saw it in Spain." He paused for a moment and drew in a breath.

"We hit them hard," Veikko said. "Made them bleed. That's what matters. I know from experience that we'll live in the heads of those pilots that survived. They'll soon spread the word to their comrades. That will make them anxious and anxious men make mistakes."

"Does it matter to the people in those buildings?" Vesa asked. "The ones still burning?"

No one answered that. The wind whistled against the walls again and the stove hissed. Snow shifted and slid from the roof with a muffled thump.

Veikko stood. "Clean your gear. We may be up again before nightfall."

Both men nodded. A looming question hung in the air: would they return?

The air-raid siren wailed like a wounded animal. The high and shrill sound was unrelenting. Veikko was already moving before the second pitch peaked. He burst from the pilot's tent with helmet in one hand and his gloves half-pulled on. His boots crunched across the frost-hardened snow. The cold slapped him awake harder than the siren ever could. Behind him, Vesa and Arttu followed without a word, the same grim urgency painted across their faces.

"Three contacts. South-southeast. Speed suggests fighters," a runner shouted as they passed, voice nearly drowned by the scream of the siren and the distant, rising rumble of engines. "Possible bombers in trail!"

The ground crew had already rolled the Fokkers out to the hard pack. Fuel lines flailed on the snow, dragged aside mid-refueling. Ammunition crates lay split open like ribs, belts half-fed into waiting guns. Mechanics were shouting to one another over the wind, tightening hatches, slapping canopies shut, and kicking blocks from under wheels.

Veikko vaulted into his cockpit, heart already hammering. He yanked on his straps, slammed the throttle forward, and cranked the primer pump. The engine coughed, choked, then roared awake in a blast of exhaust and black smoke.

He didn't wait for clearance. The D.XXI bounced across the uneven strip, tail lifting, wings biting into the sky like claws. Beside him, Vesa's aircraft leaped from the ground. Arttu was close behind. The airfield shrank behind them. The cold sky swallowed the sound.

The patrol rose fast, skimming along the treetops before leveling out just above the cloud line. The snow-covered earth stretched out beneath them. The ground was peppered with forests, both pine and birch, along with frozen lakes that glittered like shattered glass. The air was smoother at altitude, but colder, biting through layers of wool and leather.

Veikko checked his instruments, then his position. "Check in," he called over the radio.

"Haarla, tight on your wing," Vesa said.

"Koskinen, trailing ten meters back," Arttu added. "Holding speed."

"Eyes sharp. We've got visual contact reported beyond the ice fields of Lake Saimaa. Stay loose."

The wind howled outside the cockpit. The only sound in the headset was breath, static, and the occasional creak of fabric shifting over metal. Then Vesa's voice came in. His voice sounded tight and clipped, betraying his anxiety. "I've got movement. Two o'clock low. Shadow flicker under the clouds."

"Copy. Closing in."

Veikko dipped his nose, easing toward the break in the cloud line. The light was different there, thinner and grayish. A few moments later, he saw them. Three dark shapes cutting fast against the horizon. Sleek and angular. *Fighters.*

"I-16s," Veikko said. "Three of them."

"Think they've seen us?" Arttu asked.

Veikko never got the chance to answer. The sky exploded. Two more fighters dropped from above in a steep dive. The aircraft were so fast they seemed to appear out of the sun. Tracers lit the sky. Arttu's Fokker jolted, then banked hard. A second later, the radio erupted with shouts.

"I'm hit! Right wing. Summer of cunts, I'm losing—"

"Break! Break left!"

Veikko rolled hard to port, avoiding the burst aimed straight through where his tail had been a heartbeat earlier. One of the Soviet fighters snapped past him. It's movement tight, and precise. It banked to rejoin the others.

"Five total," Vesa shouted. "Three in the box, two hammering from above. They're flying like a team."

These men don't fly amateurs or conscripts. The Soviets flew together in unison. Who were they?

Veikko looked down just long enough to see Arttu's plane spiraling, smoke streaming from the fuselage. *No chute.* He sighed.

The Soviets descended like a flock of predators, striking in perfect synchronicity. They moved in perfect coordination, turning, rolling, and firing in tandem as if they shared the same mind. The three I-16s in the box swung left in a wide arc, forcing Veikko high. At the same instant, the two from above cut in under him, and raked Vesa's Fokker with withering bursts.

Tracers slashed across the sky, crossing in a perfect X. Vesa's plane caught fire mid-roll. A burst hit the fuel line.

The right wing ignited in a bright bloom of orange, and the Fokker pitched sideways, as flames crawled across the fuselage.

Veikko shouted into the mic. "Bail out, Vesa!"

No reply. Vesa's Fokker plunged through the clouds trailing fire. It didn't rise again.

Veikko jerked his head around, searching for Arttu. For a moment, he thought he saw him down low, trailing smoke, his craft nosing down in a shallow spiral.

Then the wing sheared off. A moment of silence followed. One that didn't belong in combat. Veikko felt it in his chest like a sudden vacuum, like something had been yanked from the air around him.

No chute or radio call. Just gone...

"Niemi to base," Veikko said, breathing through gritted teeth. "We've been hit. It's a coordinated strike, five fighters. Vesa and Arttu are down. Repeat: Vesa and Arttu are down."

Another burst snapped past his canopy. Veikko rolled hard, diving through a break in the cloud cover. The G-forces slammed into him. His vision narrowed as the altimeter spun. *This wasn't a mission. It was a hunt.*

The dive carried him through the clouds like a bullet through smoke. Ice formed along the edge of the windscreen. The wind howled around the frame, screaming in protest as Veikko pushed the D.XXI past its comfort zone. The altimeter spun past 1,000 meters. Then 800. Then 600.

Another burst tore past his wing, bright lines of death that vanished into the white. He leveled out just above the treetops. He was so low the snow-coated branches blurred past beneath him like river spray. His gloves slipped slightly on the stick from sweat, even through the cold.

The protocol was clear: return to altitude, regroup, await orders, but orders and protocols wouldn't save him now. He kicked the rudder and weaved between frozen ridge lines, using the terrain itself to shield his flight path. Every second he stayed in the open sky was one more second he invited steel through his engine block.

Behind him, the Soviets didn't follow. They didn't need to. Their work was done.

He risked a glance back. Nothing. Just a wash of gray clouds and cold blue sky beyond it. Empty, but it didn't feel like survival. It felt like desertion.

Veikko gritted his teeth and pushed west, keeping the tree line just beneath his wheels. He didn't feel the cold anymore. Just the weight of silence where two voices had been moments before.

The engine droned, steady and alone. Veikko kept one eye on the terrain and the other on the instruments, but his mind drifted. The rhythmic vibration of the airframe against his boots, the hiss of the wind over the canopy frame. These were the only sounds left.

No Arttu cracking jokes over the radio. No Vesa with his dry, clipped confirmations. Just the dull hum of a man flying away from the dead.

He banked gently, following a frozen river west. Below, the world was beautiful in a way that felt cruel. Pines heavy with snow. Ice glittering on the open stretches of water. Smoke curling in the far distance. It was too far to tell if it was from homes or wreckage.

They moved like a team. They didn't scatter or chase. They executed.

The thoughts came not with emotion, but with clarity. Tactical, clinical. Like counting instruments on a checklist, but underneath that, something else pressed in. Not fear or guilt.

It was absence. A cold, hard void that had settled just beneath his ribs. He adjusted the trim, hands steady, and let the Fokker ride the air.

He'd seen men die before, but never so cleanly. So quickly. It was like the Wolfpack had rehearsed it. Like they knew exactly where to aim and when to fire. The kind of strike that couldn't come from raw numbers or desperation.

It came from discipline, planning, and lots of practice. A doctrine they hadn't seen yet, but now they had. *How can I counter the strategy or at least survive it.*

The airstrip came into view over a stand of pines. The thin strip of open land was white, narrow, and rutted with fresh scars from takeoffs and landings. Smoke curled from the far end of the runway where a fuel drum had burned earlier that morning. The scent of scorched rubber and hot oil hit Veikko as soon as he dipped below treetop level. The smell cut through the cold air and swirling past the edge of his windscreen.

He throttled back, eased the flaps down, and let the nose sink. The Fokker touched down hard. Once, then again bouncing before the wheels bit into the frozen earth. The tail dipped, and the airframe rattled like a wagon full of iron. He let it roll, coasting past the empty dispersal bays where Vesa and Arttu should've parked.

He killed the engine. The sudden silence was deafening.

A ground crewman approached with hesitant steps, holding a chock in one hand. He glanced toward the horizon, as if still expecting others to follow.

"Where are—?"

Veikko flashed the maintainer a withering glare and climbed out without answering.

Command Tent – Ten Minutes Later

The canvas flap hadn't stopped moving since morning. Veikko ducked inside, helmet still under one arm, his flight suit streaked with oil and smoke. Captain Nieminen looked up from the field map spread across the table. He took one look at Veikko's face and said nothing.

Veikko stood at attention. "Lieutenant Niemi reporting. White Two and White Three lost in action to enemy fighters. Five in total. Tight maneuver and coordination between them. Three in a forward wedge, two in a high perch. Engagement lasted ninety seconds. Zero margin for counteraction."

Nieminen removed his pipe and set it down, slowly. "You're sure about the formation?"

"Yes, sir. They didn't move like individuals. They moved as one."

Nieminen shook his head. "From what I am hearing from the other bases most of the Russian pilots are incompetent fools. Wherever our planes appear, they start falling out of the sky. What curse have we earned to be inflicted with competent enemies?"

"They were beyond competent. They flew as if the planes were an extension of their bodies. It was all I could do to escape. Something was familiar about their flying, but I can't place it. Perhaps it will come to me."

The tent was quiet except for the radio's low static in the background. Somewhere outside, a mechanic dropped a wrench with a metallic clatter. No one flinched at the sudden sharp noise.

Nieminen gestured to the map. "Show me where you encountered them."

Veikko stepped forward and tapped the sheet with a gloved finger. His finger rested on a location just east of Lake Saimaa, over a thin strip of frozen forest.

"They struck here. No hesitation or verbal coordination."

Nieminen's brow furrowed. "Like a drill."

Veikko nodded. "Exactly like a drill."

Heiskanen, still manning the radio, looked up. "We lost contact with another patrol near Sortavala. Same time window."

Nieminen exhaled slowly. He reached for the pencil at the edge of the table and drew a small red X where Veikko had pointed. Then he drew another.

Captain Nieminen stared at the map a moment longer. Two red Xs. Then a third. His jaw tightened around the stem of his pipe, but he didn't light it. "You're certain they weren't communicating?" he asked.

"No radio traffic or signals. Not even wing rocks," Veikko said. "They didn't need to talk. They knew the sequence already."

Nieminen gave a slow nod, the kind of gesture that

wasn't agreement so much as acceptance of a truth he didn't like. He picked up the grease pencil again and circled the area near Veikko's mark, twice. A slow, heavy ring.

"We'll increase patrol separation," he muttered. "Double-check grid rotation schedules. And find out who in Viipuri command authorized that last recon flight."

Veikko stood silent. He had nothing left to add.

Nieminen looked up at him. "Good flying today. Under the circumstances. I'm glad you made it back."

"I brought back one plane," Veikko said. "The Soviets brought back five."

Nieminen gave a grunt. The sound was somewhere between agreement and dismissal. "That'll be all, Lieutenant."

Veikko nodded, turned on his heels, and stepped back into the cold. The tent flap slapped closed behind him, and with it, the last warmth of officialdom. Outside, the wind cut sharper than before, as if the air itself had been listening in on the report and didn't like what it heard.

He walked across the hard-packed snow in silence. His boots crunched and he had his helmet under his arm. The wind, a little stronger than earlier, tugged at the hem of his coat. The sky was pale and empty. It looked just like it had before the mission, unconcerned, unchanged, as if it hadn't taken two men with it.

The wind had picked up. The pilot's tent groaned against the gusts, the canvas bowing inward with every slap of air. Veikko stepped through the flap and stood in the threshold.

The stove had gone cold. The kettle sat empty on the

iron top, crusted with the brown ring of yesterday's tea. Arttu's gloves were still on the bench where he'd left them, one folded neatly, the other inside out. A half-eaten biscuit lay on a tin plate near Vesa's cot. The crumbs hadn't moved.

He crossed to his bunk, unstrapped his sidearm, and sat. The creak of the cot beneath him was the only sound. No one spoke. No one needed to. The absences did all the talking.

He stared at Arttu's gloves for a while. Then he reached out, turned the inside-out one right again, and laid it beside the other. He could still hear Arttu's voice. Not from the sky, but from last night, from beside the stove, from the way he'd laughed when the kettle whistled too loud and spilled steam across his hand. He remembered Vesa sipping tea in silence, rubbing his thumb over the same chipped spot on his cup, like it grounded him.

They were small things. Worthless in war. They were gone now, and the tent felt larger without them. Emptier.

A pair of boots crunched outside. Veikko stood as the flap opened again. Corporal Heiskanen poked his head in, face pinched against the wind.

"Sir, Captain Nieminen wants you in the fuel tent. A briefing has started."

Veikko nodded once. He took one last glance at the empty bunks, at the little things left behind, and stepped out without a word.

Squad Leader Briefing

The meeting was held in the fuel tent. A folding table and mismatched chairs, scavenged from supply crates and tool benches, occupied the newly swept and cleared space.

The stove in the corner rattled and popped with damp wood. A map of southern Karelia was pinned to a support post with a bayonet.

Veikko stood near the back, arms folded, and his helmet tucked under his elbow. Five other squad leaders were present, most still in flight suits. Captain Nieminen stood at the head of the table. His pipe was clenched between his teeth, and his brow furrowed deep enough to carve.

"Three ambushes," he said. "Four patrols hit in the last forty-eight hours. The enemy was always in tight maneuver groups and attacked without warning."

He pointed to the red Xs he'd marked earlier, Veikko's, Blue Flight's, and now a third near Pitkäranta.

"Same tactics?" asked Lieutenant Järvinen, a hard-bitten pilot from Lapland.

"Same execution," Veikko said. "They fly like a display team. Not just drilled. Choreographed."

"Could be ex-aerobatics pilots," another said.

Nieminen nodded. "Or someone trained by them."

Veikko stepped forward and rested a hand on the map. "It's not a large group. Five planes. Maybe six. But they're not choosing random patrols. They're striking sectors just as we commit rotation. That means someone's studying our flight patterns."

There was a beat of silence. Wind scraped across the canvas above them like fingernails on a drum skin. Lieutenant Järvinen asked the question no one wanted to.

"You think they're hunting us?"

Veikko looked him in the eye. "They're not just hunting. They're learning."

A long silence followed. The stove popped. Somewhere outside, a muffled engine coughed to life, then sputtered out.

Lieutenant Soini, the youngest of the group, cleared his throat. "They're not hitting our supply convoys. Not striking our fuel depots. Just patrols and of course, the pilots that fly them."

Nieminen nodded slowly. "Because we're the only threat that can reach them before they drop their payloads. Take out enough of us, and they fly with impunity."

"They're not targeting kills at random," Veikko added. "They're prioritizing our lead elements, wing leaders, and flight commanders. Every strike has followed a consistent pattern: remove the threat and retreat clean."

"They haven't lost a single aircraft," said Järvinen.

No one spoke after that. Nieminen walked to the edge of the table and picked up the teapot and poured black tea into a dented mug. He didn't drink it. He just held it between both hands and stared down into the steam.

Then he said, "I want their pattern broken."

Veikko straightened. "I think it can be done, but not by reacting."

"Go on."

"They're used to initiative. We need to fake a rotation gap. Draw them into a sector that looks exposed. Bait them in with an intentionally thinned patrol. Maybe a pair of green flyers or pilots acting like they're green. Then hold a shadow element above and behind the bait group. High perch, radio silent."

"You want to reverse the trap?" Nieminen asked.

Veikko nodded. "It's the only way to see how they move from a vantage. And the only way to take out a coordinated unit is to force them into improvisation."

"And the green flyers?"

Veikko didn't blink. "They have to survive long enough to bait the strike. That's the risk."

Järvinen shifted uncomfortably in his seat. "And who do we send to fly the trap?"

Veikko didn't hesitate. "I'll lead it. I owe the bastards for Arttu and Vesa."

Captain Nieminen said nothing for a long moment. The steam from his untouched tea drifted upward, curling into the stale air of the tent. The wind rattled the canvas again, more insistent now, like it was trying to get in.

At last, he gave a slow nod. "Approved," he said. "We'll set the trap tomorrow. Dawn patrol sector Delta-Two. I'll notify Viipuri Command to delay their rotation cycle by an hour. That should leave the corridor just exposed enough."

He looked at Veikko. "Pick your shadow element. Three pilots experienced only. Keep the rest grounded."

Veikko inclined his head. "Understood."

"You'll have a new wingman by nightfall," Nieminen added, setting the mug down with a dull ceramic clack. "Fresh transfer from Utti. Arrived an hour ago."

Veikko raised an eyebrow. "Name?"

Nieminen took a clipboard from a pile near the stove and flipped through several smudged sheets. "Senior Warrant Officer Ilmari Kuusela. Flew recon out of Lappeenranta before the war. One confirmed kill during border skirmishes. No squadron experience. Rated competent by his last CO."

Veikko didn't react. Not visibly.

Järvinen gave a dry snort. "Throwing the new blood to the wolves already?"

Nieminen didn't smile. "We're out of wolves. All we have left are the pups."

The room fell quiet again.

Veikko nodded once. "I'll meet him."

Mess Tent – Evening

The mess tent stank of boiled potatoes, damp wool, and too many bodies packed into too little space. Tin trays clattered, boots thudded against the canvas floor, and now and then someone laughed too loudly, as if noise alone could drown out the memory of what the airfield had sounded like that morning. The heat from the stove in the center couldn't quite chase the chill from the corners, and the smoke curling near the ceiling gave the air a sour, metallic taste that clung to the back of the throat.

Veikko moved down the line with his tray, accepting a scoop of gray stew without comment. He passed the stove in the center, surrounded by pilots and ground crew alike, and spotted a new face at the end of one of the benches. Young, sharp-featured, with windburn along the cheekbones and a distant stare that didn't quite match the casual grip he had on his tea. *That must be Senior Warrant Officer Ilmari Kuusela.*

He wasn't talking. Just listening. Two mechanics were spinning a story about a bomb that had failed to go off earlier in the day, something about a fuel drum, a snowbank, and divine luck. Kuusela offered a polite smile, but didn't laugh. His tray sat untouched.

Veikko sat across from him without asking.

Kuusela looked up, met his eyes, and gave a nod. "Sir."

Veikko gestured at the tray. "Not hungry?"

"Hard to eat," Kuusela said, "when every name you're hoping to hear just turns into silence."

Veikko studied him for a moment. No fidgeting. No empty chatter. He wasn't green but he wasn't tested either. Not yet. "You fly out of Utti?" Veikko asked.

Kuusela nodded. "Mostly recon. Short hops. Kept the camera warm more than the guns."

"And your last CO called you competent."

Kuusela gave a ghost of a smile. "That sounds like him."

Veikko set down his spoon. "We fly at dawn."

"I figured."

"You'll be on my wing."

Kuusela didn't flinch. He didn't beam, either. He just gave another nod and picked up his spoon. Veikko watched him for another second, then stood and left his tray behind.

Outside – Later That Night

Snow fell in thin flurries, more drifting than descending. The airfield had gone quiet, just the occasional clang of a tool in the motor pool or the murmur of a sentry's footsteps crunching along the perimeter.

Veikko walked the flight line alone, his coat pulled tight. The Fokkers were dark shapes under canvas wraps, skeletal in the moonlight. Somewhere to the south, artillery rumbled like distant thunder. The fires in the city had been put out. The green ribbon of the Aurora Borealis danced in the sky above.

The names still hadn't stopped vanishing from his mind. Names of the men who were under his command. Men who no longer drew breath. *My responsibility. My fault.*

He paused near Arttu's bay. The wheel chocks still sat where the ground crew had left them, untouched. Frost had grown along the edges. He turned toward the wind, inhaled once, and let it cut clean through him.

Chapter 4

Forward Airfield, Outside Viipuri

December 1, 1939

The cold was sharper before dawn. It bit through wool and canvas and leather as if nothing existed between skin and the open sky. Each breath burned in the lungs, thin and dry, leaving a taste of iron on the back of the tongue.

Lieutenant Veikko Niemi pulled his flight cap tighter and ducked his head against the wind as he strode toward the hard pack where the Fokkers waited. Their shapes loomed under canvas covers that were white with frost. The Fokker's propellers glinted faintly under the pale wash of stars.

The airfield lights were doused. Only lanterns shielded by canvas hoods threw small pools of yellow across the snow. Men moved quickly and quietly. There were no shouts or unnecessary words. Even the mechanics, hauling fuel drums and straining to pull frozen belts into machine guns, worked with a grim, silent urgency.

"Your orders have been confirmed, sir," said Corporal

Heiskanen, falling in step beside him. "Visual patrol sector Alpha-One. Soviet bomber group spotted heading northwest across Lake Ladoga."

"Fighters?"

"Scouts report four, maybe six, ahead of the main body. Speed's light. Could be protecting the bombers."

Veikko grunted. He already knew what they'd find: lumbering SB-2s flying low and tight, with Polikarpov fighters stitched around them like angry dogs.

Ahead, he spotted the pilots forming up, Senior Warrant Officer Ilmari Kuusela, and two others: Sergeant Aarni Virtanen and Sergeant Matti Rautio, both from the neighboring 26th Squadron. Kuusela caught Veikko's eye and gave a small nod. He appeared calm and composed. No false bravado or wide grins. Just readiness. *Good.*

Veikko climbed into the cockpit, the leather seat hard and bitterly cold against his thighs. He worked the primer pump one, two, three times, and jammed the throttle forward. The Fokker's engine coughed, sputtered, and then caught with a hard, barking roar. Exhaust plumed into the dark like steam from some hidden furnace.

One by one, the others came alive beside him, their engines rolling into a steady, defiant growl. Veikko adjusted his harness and keyed the mic. "Formation check."

"Kuusela, on your wing."

"Virtanen, right echelon."

"Rautio, trail position."

He smiled grimly. *Tight and by the book. Good.*

"Stay loose," he said. "If they scatter, don't chase. Bombers are the priority."

"Understood," came the crackled replies.

He taxied into position, nose pointing north. The hard pack runway stretched into the darkness, barely visible. Beyond it, the empty sky waited, flat and pale.

He pushed the throttle forward and felt the Fokker lurch. The plane picked up speed as it rolled toward the end of the runway. The tires kissed the frozen ground once, then twice, and then he was airborne. He rose into the colorless void where day hadn't yet begun. *Another day. Another fight. The Soviets thought they could take the sky. They were wrong.*

The first light of day broke slow and sullen across the eastern horizon. No sunrise, only a thinning of the darkness. A gray that bled across the treetops and froze the clouds in a flat iron sheet overhead. The ground below was a fractured mirror of snow and ice. The frozen lakes stitched together by dark threads of forest.

Veikko leveled off at two thousand meters and pulled into a wide search pattern. The cold seeped through the seams of his flight jacket, biting harder than the climb had. He adjusted his trim and scanned the haze where the Ladoga ice fields spread like a battered shield.

Minutes passed. The headset crackled faintly with static. Then Kuusela's voice cut through, low and calm. "Visual. Ten o'clock low. Multiple contacts. Heavy types."

Veikko craned his neck, catching a flicker against the gray horizon. Dark shapes moved over the white, steady and slow. The contact appeared first as specks, then grew larger with each passing moment until the black dots morphed into planes with wide wings, twin engines that glinted with frost.

"Confirm bombers," Veikko said. "Six at least."

"No sign of fighters yet," Kuusela added. "But they're there. Bet on it."

Veikko keyed the mic again. "Hold formation. Climb for advantage. We strike from above."

He eased the nose higher and felt the Fokker respond with a soft resistance. The others mirrored his movement. Their response was tight, clean, and disciplined. *Excellent.*

As they gained altitude, he saw it: three smaller shadows weaving just above the bombers, their stubby wings and quick movements betraying them.

"Fighter escort confirmed," Veikko said. "I-16s. Three visible. Assume more."

The Polikarpovs flew loose, casual, almost lazy in their weaving pattern. *Too confident. Good.*

Veikko keyed the mic once more, his voice even. "We go in two flights. I'll lead the initial pass on the bombers. Kuusela, with me. Virtanen and Rautio sweep the top. Keep the fighters busy."

A chorus of affirmatives crackled back. He rolled his shoulders once, loosening the tension that had already gathered under the harness straps. *Targets in sight. Formation holding. Time to show them the sky wasn't theirs yet.*

Veikko pushed the stick forward, tilting the nose into a shallow dive. The Fokker responded instantly, the engine pitch rising to a strained, and eager whine. Below, the Soviet bombers continued their crawl westward. Blissfully unaware that death was already folding in from above.

"Throttle to climb speed," Veikko barked over the mic. "We hit and climb. No second passes unless clean."

He angled for the center of the bomber formation. He picked out the lead aircraft, a broad-shouldered SB-2 running slightly ahead of the others, likely the pathfinder. Kuusela slid into place on his wing, silent and steady.

Veikko squinted through the frost-caked gunsight. The bomber filled his view, silver under the ice crystals, dark green on the upper fuselage, the red star stark on the tail. He could see the dorsal gunner beginning to swivel. *Too late.*

Veikko thumbed the trigger. The Brownings snarled. Tracer rounds stitched across the sky, a tight, rising arc that punched through the bomber's left engine nacelle. The SB-2's wing shuddered and fuel sprayed out in a mist that ignited in a bright flash.

The enemy bomber yawed violently as it dipped a wing. Smoke and flames poured from the torn engine. Veikko yanked back on the stick, climbing hard, bullets slicing through the air beneath him as the bomber's tail gunner sprayed wildly.

"Direct hit," Kuusela's voice came, clipped and professional.

Veikko caught a flash of movement to his right, Kuusela's Fokker rolling into a dive on a second bomber. His guns flared, short, controlled bursts. The second SB-2's glass nose shattered like brittle ice. The bomber shuddered and lost altitude fast, smoke billowing from its forward fuselage.

Above them, Virtanen and Rautio engaged the fighter escort. Short bursts of gunfire crackled through the thin air. Veikko caught glimpses of I-16s twisting and rolling, trying to respond, but they were scattered, uncoordinated. *This wasn't the Wolfpack. This was something they could kill.*

Veikko leveled out, scanning for a fresh target. Below, the Soviet formation was in chaos, bombers veered off course, as they tried to tighten into defensive formations, but it was too late.

He keyed his mic. "Finish it."

Virtanen struck first. His Fokker dove through the defensive arc of one of the escorting I-16s, snapping off a clean burst that tore through the Polikarpov's rear fuselage. The Soviet fighter wobbled, tried to climb, then nosed over and spun into the clouds like a discarded toy.

"Splash one," Virtanen called, surprised by how quickly the enemy fighter broke apart.

Rautio wasn't far behind. His guns flared, raking a bomber that had broken wide to the east. As the SB-2's fuselage separated from its left wing, the wing crumpled inward, spraying debris. The bomber staggered sideways, caught air for a second, and then fell. The wounded beast cartwheeled through the lower cloud layer in a slow, smoking spiral.

Above the fight, the surviving I-16s pulled into a frantic, haphazard climb as they scattered like startled birds. They had no interest in staying now. Their screen broken, their bombers falling, they fled east toward the gray smudge of the Ladoga horizon.

Veikko leveled out high above the burning wreckage below, breathing hard through the mask of frost on his scarf. "Regroup," he said into the mic. "We're done here."

Kuusela's voice came back, steady. "On your wing."

"Virtanen. Rautio. Status?"

"Both green," Virtanen said. "Rautio's leaking a little, but flight capable."

"Good."

They turned west, into the rising light, leaving the shattered formation behind them.

The flight back was quiet. The wind whined over the wings, and the engines hummed steady and low. No chatter on the radio. No boasts. Just the steady grind of propellers pushing them home through the brittle morning air.

Below, the snowfields blurred past scarred now by fresh craters and burned-out wrecks barely visible through the gray haze. The airfield came into view after twenty minutes. A strip of battered hard pack dug into the frozen earth. Thin smoke curled from the fuel drums near the southern edge, but the runway was clear. The ground crews were already lined up, watching, waiting.

Veikko led the descent, his Fokker shuddering slightly as the landing gear locked into place. He touched down hard, no ceremony or finesse as his wheels bit the frozen ground. His taunt shoulder muscles relaxed as the plane jolted with the thump of survival.

Kuusela followed neatly behind. Virtanen and Rautio came in slower. Rautio's plane trailed a faint, lazy streamer of smoke from the wing but held firm.

They taxied to the dispersal line. Their engines sputtered to silence, one by one. The sudden stillness settled over the field like a blanket, broken only by the soft hiss of cooling metal.

Veikko climbed down stiffly. His knees ached from the cold and strain. As he pulled off his flight helmet, a blast of freezing wind slapped his face, bringing the smells of burnt oil and damp canvas with it.

He looked once over the field, at the tents, waiting crews, and the empty sky beyond. *They had won today. But the sky wasn't theirs. Not yet.*

Chapter 5

Forward Airfield, Outside Viipuri

December 1, 1939

The message came in broken and raw, carried on a wave of static that made the canvas walls tremble. Corporal Heiskanen hunched over the radio set, one hand gripping the dial. The other scribbled down what words he could catch on a stained notepad.

His face was pale. The pencil jerked each time the signal cracked and faded. Veikko stood behind him, arms folded, as he listened through the static roar. "—request recovery team—coordinates—eastern sector—three aircraft down—no enemy contact—repeat, no enemy contact—"

The transmission fizzled, hissed, and snapped out. Captain Nieminen pulled the headphones off Heiskanen's head and placed them around his own ears. He twisted the tuning dial with careful precision, but no further signal came through. Just the low hum of the atmosphere.

"Three Soviet fighters were downed," Nieminen said quietly, setting the headphones down. "No enemy contact reported."

Heiskanen glanced up, hesitating. "Sir, they sounded confused and panicked."

"They were ambushed," Veikko said, the certainty solid in his voice. "And they don't even know how."

Nieminen turned to him, brow furrowing. "You think it's the same group?"

"I don't think. I know." Veikko stepped forward, tapped the map still pinned against the table. "Here. Eastern patrol sectors. Isolated flights. Small group movements."

He jabbed his finger at the paths crisscrossing the region.

"They're picking off our patrols the same way they just gutted their own."

Järvinen, standing near the stove, spoke up. "Why would they turn on their own aircraft?"

"They didn't," Veikko said. "Those I-16s weren't collaborating. They were flying separately. Sloppy. Easy targets. Whoever leads this group doesn't tolerate weakness. Even among their own so he taught them a lesson."

The tent was silent, save for the faint crackle of the dying fire in the stove. Veikko rested both hands on the edge of the table, leaning in. "I read a dispatch once," he said, voice low. "From the Atlantic. German submarines operating off the British coast. They don't hunt alone anymore. They run in packs. The group circle convoys, to isolate the weak. Then they strike fast and vanish before anyone can respond."

He tapped the map again, more gently this time. "That's what this is. Fighters instead of subs, sky instead of ocean but the method is the same."

Captain Nieminen's pipe stem clicked softly against his teeth as he chewed over the idea. "A wolfpack," Nieminen said at last.

Veikko nodded once. "That's what we're fighting. Not a patrol or a squadron. A pack."

The name settled in the tent like smoke, heavy, and inevitable. No one argued.

"I still don't understand why they would kill their own brothers," Järvinen said.

Captain Nieminen's eyes narrowed. "They're cleaning their own lines."

Veikko nodded once. "They're sharpening the blade before they turn it back on us."

Captain Nieminen leaned over the map again, the lamplight catching the deep lines carved into his face. "I wonder who is leading this group? I thought anyone worth a damn over there was killed in the purges," he said quietly.

Veikko didn't hesitate. "I thought about it last night. The flying style seemed familiar, and then it came to me, Major Grigori Chernyavin."

Järvinen looked up sharply. "The Red Star team leader?"

"The same," Veikko confirmed, his voice tightening.

His left shoulder throbbed with the phantom pain that always accompanied thoughts of the Soviet ace. "I've faced him before, in Spain. My first combat mission."

Nieminen's eyebrows rose. "You never mentioned that."

Veikko's jaw clenched briefly. "Not much to tell. He shot me down like I was a novice straight from flight school. Which I was." He traced a finger over the map, following the attack patterns they'd documented. "But I spent weeks in a hospital bed afterward studying his tactics. The way he isolates his target. The way he forces defensive maneuvers he's already prepared to counter."

He looked up, meeting Nieminen's gaze. "Two years ago, I watched him through my canopy as I spiraled toward the ground. I swore if I ever saw him again, I'd be ready and now he's here."

Nieminen studied him for a long moment. "This is personal for you."

"It's professional," Veikko corrected, but his eyes betrayed him. "Though I won't deny I've thought about settling the score since that day in Spain."

He jabbed two fingers against the edge of the table. "They weren't just performers. They were trainers. Hundreds of Soviet fighter pilots learned his formations before the war."

Nieminen's brow furrowed deeper. "I thought he was killed in the purges."

"Rumors," Veikko said. "No proof. Just whispers. I don't think Chernyavin vanished. I think he spent some time in one of their re-education camps."

He tapped the three red Xs Nieminen had marked on the map, the lost patrols, the broken formations, the quiet disappearances. "This isn't just random skill. It's discipline under one hand. Every attack we've suffered follows a rehearsal structure. There's no panic. No improvisation. Only calculated, cold precision."

He straightened and looked Nieminen in the eye. "Chernyavin is still alive. And he's leading them."

The wind battered the side of the tent again, the sound like claws raking across canvas. For the first time, Veikko thought he saw something like uncertainty flicker across Nieminen's face. Only for a second. Then it was gone, replaced by the grim, familiar mask of command.

"If he's alive," Nieminen said, "we'll drag him out of his den."

Veikko nodded once. "We'll need the right bait. The Wolfpack is out there. Let's implement the plan we discussed."

Captain Nieminen straightened, tapping the map lightly with the end of his pencil. "Sector Delta-Two," he said. "Early rotation schedule. Gaps in patrol coverage wide enough to tempt a confident group."

He looked across the tent at Heiskanen, who was already scribbling notes onto a pad.
"Send a dummy signal to Viipuri Command," Nieminen ordered. "Have them adjust grid traffic to make Delta-Two look vulnerable. No mention of a trap."

Heiskanen nodded sharply. "Yes, sir."

Veikko stepped closer to the table, studying the terrain features. Forests, frozen lakes, thin cloud cover expected over the morning hours. *Enough to hide an approach but thin enough to maintain line of sight during engagement.*

"I'll lead the shadow flight," Veikko said. "Kuusela stays on my wing."

Nieminen's eyes flicked up. "You trust him? After just one flight with you?"

"I trust his discipline," Veikko said. "He'll follow orders. He won't chase glory."

Nieminen grunted. "Good. Pick two others from the pool. Experienced hands only. No one with fewer than twenty sorties."

"I already have names," Veikko said.

"Then get moving," Nieminen said. He reached down and scratched a match along the table edge, relighting his pipe with slow, deliberate motions. The first draw glowed red in the dim lantern light.

"We spring the trap this afternoon," Nieminen said around the pipe stem. "No more ghosts. No more guessing. Either we bring them down or we find out who comes back."

Veikko saluted crisply. He turned and stepped out into the wind. The canvas flap slapped shut behind him as the brittle light of a hard, cold day closed over the field.

Chapter 6

Midday,

Flight Line

December 1st, 1939

The sun hung low over the horizon, casting long, pale shadows across the hard-packed snow. The air smelled of cold oil, frost, and the iron tang of yesterday's smoke. A brittle wind skimmed across the airfield, stirring the loose snow into thin shifting veils that scraped against the battered tents and the wings of the waiting aircraft. Everything looked frozen in place, silent, and waiting, like the world itself was holding its breath.

Veikko strode toward the dispersal line where the Fokkers waited. Several of the planes had their canvas covers pulled back, as the mechanics worked to fast prep the aircraft for a rapid launch. The ground crews moved with the same silent urgency as always.

He spotted Kuusela first, standing beside his Fokker, helmet tucked under his arm, already watching the sky. "Briefing, now," Veikko barked.

Virtanen and Rautio joined them a moment later, their faces drawn but focused. *Good. No need for a second team.*

They huddled behind the nearest aircraft, Veikko speaking low and fast. "We fly two sections. Bait and blade. Virtanen and Rautio, you're the bait."

He jabbed a finger toward the south. "You'll fly a standard patrol loop near Delta-Two. Nothing fancy. Maintain tight line abreast formation, broadcast on standard frequencies and make it look real."

Virtanen grimaced but nodded. "Understood."

"Kuusela and I will stay high and silent, shadowing you from the west at two thousand meters. No radio traffic unless attacked. Maintain radio silence otherwise."

Rautio shifted uneasily. "And if they hit hard?"

"You stay alive long enough for us to strike," Veikko said. His voice was flat. No softening or comfort. They all knew what bait meant.

Veikko looked at Kuusela. "If we see movement, we strike their leader first. Don't chase the stragglers. We shatter the head, and the body falls apart."

Kuusela nodded once, sharp and mechanical. "Copy."

A mechanic waved from the fueling truck, signaling that all aircraft were ready.

Veikko pulled his gloves tight and stepped back, surveying his flight.

"Let's make them regret showing their teeth," he said.

Without another word, they turned and climbed into their cockpits. The sky waited and this time, they weren't flying blind.

Delta-Two Sector – Early Afternoon

The air was brutally still above the frozen forests. Lieutenant Veikko Niemi leveled out at two thousand meters, his Fokker's engine thrumming steadily in the brittle cold. He scanned the empty sky to the east, the sun a thin smear of light behind a screen of high, dirty clouds. Below, less than a thousand meters off the deck, the bait patrol flew their pattern.

Virtanen and Rautio held a tight line abreast formation, their silhouettes cutting small, dark shapes against the broken white of the snowfields. Their movements were precise and deliberate. They flew in a predictable, textbook flying style that any Soviet recon team would recognize immediately. Just another Finnish patrol, another ripe target.

Veikko keyed his mic to Kuusela only once. "Shadow position. Maintain radio silence unless engaged."

A crackle of static, then Kuusela's voice, low and clipped: "Copy."

They arced wide, pacing the bait patrol from high and west, and staying well out of visual range. If the Wolfpack was nearby, and Veikko knew they were, he needed to look like nothing more than another wandering patrol leader.

The Fokker's controls were stiff with cold. Ice crystals spiderwebbed along the edge of the windscreen. Veikko's breath condensed in slow clouds inside his mask. He flexed his fingers once inside his gloves, settling deeper into the seat.

Time seemed to stretch. First five minutes passed and then ten. Each minute felt like an eternity of anxiety and fear dancing through their minds.

Below, Virtanen and Rautio continued their standard intercept grid. It started with a straight run that ended in a slow banking turn. Then back in the opposite direction. Virtanen and Rautio hit the perfect balance with their flying. They flew with just enough variation to avoid suspicion, but not enough to look aggressive.

Veikko's eyes never left the haze to the east. He knew how this would look to the Wolfpack. Two Finnish fighters exposed and alone flying straight into an empty sky. *Perfect bait.*

He checked his instruments again. He felt a slight tremble against the rising afternoon crosswinds. *Still nothing.*

The sky stretched out pale and heartless around them, and the snowfields below glittered like broken glass. Virtanen and Rautio played the part of the lamb well. Somewhere out there, circling unseen, were the wolves.

The first glint came from the east. A flash of light, low on the horizon. Where the cloud cover thinned to a dirty smear. Brief enough it could have been a trick of the sun on ice, but Veikko knew better.

He pressed his boot lightly against the rudder, banking his Fokker a fraction to the right. His goggles narrowed the glare, sharpening the view. *Movement.*

Three shapes, small and fast, flickered against the clouds, there and gone, before slipping back into the murk. Veikko didn't need a second look. He recognized them for what they were. *Fighters, climbing hard.*

He keyed the mic twice. His radio emitted two sharp bursts of static and then fell silent again. It was the signal Kuusela, and the others would recognize: enemy contact, hold position, await engagement.

Below, Virtanen and Rautio kept flying their grid, oblivious by all appearances. No change in altitude or shift in their path. Just steady, routine patrol sweeps across the snow-blasted landscape.

The glints reappeared. They were higher now and arcing in widely around. *They were taking their time. Like experienced predators, they patiently executed their approach to the prey.*

Veikko could almost feel their eyes on the bait patrol below and their minds probing, weighing, and judging. Should they attack? It would be any moment now.

He tightened his gloves. His thumb rested near the trigger guard as his heart thrummed in his chest, the beat steady. *The wolves were here. Now all that remained was whether they would bite.*

A moment later they bit. The Wolfpack broke from the clouds in a perfect synchronized dive. Their formation was tight and shallow, two in the lead, one above to cover. Tracers lanced out even before they closed the distance, ripping thin lines of fire across the frozen sky.

Virtanen saw them at the last second. "Contacts! High—" His voice crackled over the open frequency, cut off in mid-call.

Veikko caught the flash of muzzle fire from the I-16s as they slashed in. Rautio rolled hard right, breaking formation instinctively, but it was too late to mask their intent. *The trap was sprung.*

Veikko jammed his throttle forward, feeling the Fokker lurch as it dug for speed. His stomach pressed against the seat harness as he pulled into a shallow dive. "Engage!" he barked over the mic. "Kuusela, on me!"

The Wolfpack pressed their advantage. One of the Soviet fighters latched onto Rautio's tail, his guns spitting. Rautio jinked left and right, trying to shake him. Smoke trailed from a crease in his wingtip.

Above it all, like a conductor lurking behind a curtain, another shape circled above the melee, the command ship. Veikko spotted him immediately. The leader didn't join the first strike. Instead, he hovered and guided the attack. The enemy kept their formation tight. *Chernyavin. It had to be.*

Veikko pushed the nose of the Fokker over as he lined up for a high-speed dive straight into the heart of the melee. "Kuusela, cover me! I'm going for their alpha!"

"Copy!" came the immediate reply.

Wind shrieked past the windscreen and ice rattled across the fuselage. The world compressed into the thin space between the lead Soviet fighter and Veikko's gunsight.

The wolves had circled the bait. They wove their attack with deadly precision, certain of the kill. Unknown to them, they weren't the only predators in the sky today. Now the hunter was coming for them. They dove from above with guns ready. A blade aimed straight for the heart of the pack.

Veikko centered the lead Soviet fighter in his sights. The I-16 rolled instinctively, sensing danger, but too late. Veikko squeezed the trigger. His Brownings chattered, stitching a tight stream of fire across the Polikarpov's fuselage.

The fighter shuddered under the impact. Smoke burst from the engine cowling. It dipped violently to the left, breaking formation and falling into a slow, trailing spiral toward the forest below. *One down.*

The remaining Soviets reacted instantly, too disciplined to panic, but visibly rattled. Their formation cracked open, and hesitation rippled through their lines. Veikko pulled hard into a climbing turn as he searched for the leader. The shadow that circled just beyond the fight. *There.*

Chernyavin's I-16 held station high and aloof. His wings were perfectly level, and his engine purred. No weaving or erratic bursts of speed. Just observation, cold and clinical.

Veikko felt a grim satisfaction twist in his chest. He sees me now.

Kuusela swung in on Veikko's six, holding formation like a shadow. "Contacts splitting. They're adjusting."

"Good," Veikko snapped. "Force them to think."

He leveled out and dove again. He wasn't aiming for the scattered fighters, but for the space they were trained to defend. There was an invisible structure to their flying.

If he could tear a hole wide enough, Chernyavin would be forced to act. The key wasn't killing them all. The key was breaking the dance.

Veikko rolled into a shallow dive as he lined up on the loose center of the shattered Soviet pattern. The surviving I-16s twisted in confusion, trying to re-form the defensive net, but the gap had already opened. *Too wide and messy.*

They were reacting now, not moving as one, but as individuals. Exactly what Veikko needed. He aimed for the weakest seam between two fighters and fired a short, brutal burst. Tracers snapped across the empty air, forcing one Soviet to roll hard left. This caused him to open up some distance from his wingman.

The formation cracked further, now a messy sprawl instead of a clean strike group. Out of the corner of his eye, Veikko saw movement. The lead I-16. The one that had circled above, silent until now, peeled into a dive. *Chernyavin.*

The Soviet ace moved like a blade, falling fast through the air without hesitation or wasted motion. His angle was clean, deliberate, diving not at Veikko, but at Kuusela's Fokker, as he aimed to cut Veikko's wing apart. *Predictable,* Veikko thought.

He yanked the stick hard right, breaking his own dive, shifting sideways into Chernyavin's attack vector. The G-forces slammed him into the seat. The force caused the Fokker to groan under the sudden stress.

Crosshairs danced across the windscreen. He squeezed the trigger. *Missed.*

Chernyavin jinked at the last instant, slipping past Veikko's burst with the kind of reflexes only a lifetime of flying could teach. He didn't panic or make the mistake to climb which would have killed his air speed and made him an easy target. Instead, he rolled inverted, diving even harder.

Kuusela rolled away, staying clear but not engaging yet. Just as Veikko had ordered. The fight was now Veikko against Chernyavin. No formation or team. Just two hunters stalking each other and only one would survive.

Veikko kicked the rudder hard, swinging his nose after Chernyavin's dive. The Soviet ace didn't bolt or run. Instead, he looped under the fight, using the frozen horizon as a shield, climbing back up into a vertical barrel roll that forced Veikko to follow or lose him entirely.

The Fokker strained, airframe shuddering as Veikko yanked into the climb. Ice cracked along the wheel struts. His breath rasped inside the flight mask.

For a split second, Veikko's gunsight framed Chernyavin's tail. He fired a short and measured burst. *Too far.*

Chernyavin rolled inverted again and dropped his nose. He slipped into a high-G descending spiral that whipped them both toward the lower cloud band. Veikko followed, the Fokker shuddered from the pressure that built across the wings, as the air thickened around them. Veikko's world narrowed into gray and white. The ground was cloaked in a curtain of swirling mist.

Visibility collapsed in an instant, the cold damp air clawing at the windscreen, turning everything into a smearing blur. It was a dangerous game, fighting blind, trusting instinct and speed instead of sight. Chernyavin didn't hesitate, and neither could Veikko.

Veikko couldn't see anything. Snow and ice blurred the world into white noise. He didn't blink. He pulled tighter and jammed his throttle to the stop. The Fokker bucked and shivered as he forced it through the spiral, trying to match the Soviet pilot's path.

Out of the mist, muzzle flashes bloomed. Chernyavin had reversed. He wasn't running. He was baiting the turn. Tracers tore past Veikko's left wingtip, chewing empty air.

Veikko broke left, hard and violent, feeling the

Fokker's frame groan under the sudden shift. One burst, then a second, and the Soviet guns fell silent. *He's either spent his ammo or is repositioning.*

Veikko climbed, banking wide. He understood now. Chernyavin didn't fly like a duelist. He flew like a surgeon. Cut, bleed, retreat, and repeat. Wearing down the enemy second by second.

Veikko steadied the climb and pulled high above the cloud layer again. Suddenly, he was awash in sunlight and was blind for several moments. Chernyavin came after him.

The Soviet ace pulled into a perfect vertical climb. His nose pointed at Veikko's tail, and guns flared in tight, controlled bursts. *Precise,* Veikko thought grimly. *Too precise.*

Veikko hauled the stick back and kicked his right rudder. His Fokker slipped sideways out of the guns' cone. A trick he learned flying against the Russians in Spain. *Always move off the axis, never pull straight.*

Chernyavin's burst missed by a finger's breadth. Now they were almost vertical, hammering skyward in a brutal climbing spiral, as energy bled from both planes. The first one to falter would fall.

Veikko gritted his teeth against the G-force. Frost crackled across the windscreen edges. The altimeter spun, the world grew smaller and narrower as he fought to remain conscious. He knew Chernyavin was better at clean execution, but Veikko wasn't playing clean anymore.

He pushed the stick forward and snapped into a brutal negative-G dive. Flipping onto its back, the Fokker entered a near free-fall. The world blurred.

A cold stabbing sensation pierced his spine as his head

throbbed with blood. Chernyavin reacted a second too late. The Soviet fighter overshot the top of the climb. This left him alone and exposed.

Veikko leveled, throttled up, and came up under Chernyavin's belly. *One chance for a clean shot.*

Veikko steadied the Fokker under Chernyavin's silhouette. Every muscle in his body was strung tight, and his instincts screaming for precision. The Soviet ace's I-16 floated ahead of him. Chernyavin was exposed for a breath. The underside of his plane's fuselage stark against the broken light filtering through the clouds.

Veikko squeezed the trigger and the Brownings roared. The first burst stitched across Chernyavin's right wing and punched ragged holes through the fabric and steel. The second ripped into the fuselage just behind the engine cowling. Black smoke poured out immediately, trailing back in a greasy ribbon across the sky.

Chernyavin's fighter lurched, staggered, and dropped a wing. For a heartbeat, Veikko thought the Soviet might recover. That he might somehow wrestle the wounded machine back through sheer will. But then the I-16 rolled over and slipped into a sharp fall, smoke trailing from its torn fuselage.

Veikko pulled up slightly, keeping his guns trained, ready to finish it. Suddenly the Soviet ace jerked the crippled fighter into a desperate, ugly roll. It wasn't clean flying or beautiful. It was survival.

Chernyavin fought the stick, forcing the damaged aircraft to stabilize into a shallow, ragged dive. Black smoke still poured from the stricken engine, but the Soviet kept control. His nose was down, he was bleeding altitude fast, but he kept the plane under control.

Veikko dropped his nose, ready to pursue, but Kuusela's voice cut through the static, sharp and urgent. "Multiple contacts. Reinforcements inbound! Bearing east!"

Veikko's eyes flicked to the horizon. He could make out two new dots, which morphed into four as they drew nearer. More Soviet fighters cutting across the cloud layer, heading straight for them. The Wolfpack was calling for its less capable cousins.

Veikko ground his teeth, weighing it for half a second. *One more clean shot and it would be over, but it was a suicide run now. Too far and exposed. He would not trade his life for a maybe. Not today.*

"Disengage," Veikko snapped. "Kuusela, with me. Pull west."

He banked hard, dragging the Fokker into a wide, fast turn away from the burning Soviet machine.
Chernyavin's wounded fighter disappeared into the haze, as it limped eastward. Smoke curled in his wake like a scar across the sky. He had survived, for now, but his Wolfpack had been broken.

Veikko throttled up, feeling the Fokker shudder under the surge of power. The engine roared against the brittle air. The sound tore across the frozen sky. He didn't look back. There was nothing left behind him but smoke, blood, and the bitter taste of a fight unfinished. The distance widened with every second, stretching out the space between survival and regret, until the eastern horizon was just a smear of gray and memory.

Chapter 7

Forward Airfield, Outside Viipuri

December 1, 1939

The landing gear hit hard, bouncing once before the tires bit into the frozen earth. Veikko rode the Fokker down the battered strip, the rudder twitching under his boots as he fought the crosswind. The engine coughed once, then settled into a low, grudging growl.

He taxied toward the dispersal line without waiting for a signal. Behind him, Kuusela's Fokker followed, trailing a faint streamer of exhaust but otherwise intact. The ground crews moved toward them at a cautious jog without any frantic waves or shouts. They knew by now what a fast landing without radio chatter meant.

Bad news or worse. Veikko killed the engine. The

sudden silence hit harder than the cold. He pulled his flight helmet off and tossed it onto the seat. He slid down the wing with the practiced motion of a man who hadn't realized how much tension he was carrying until it was gone.

Once on the ground, he leaned up against his plane and closed his eyes. He drew in a long breath and let it out slowly. *That could have gone either way. Will it be me next time trying to recover from damage? Will I be as lucky as Chernyavin or will my days end in a fireball?*

Kuusela climbed down a few meters away. His face was drawn and pale under the frost caked into his scarf. He nodded once to Veikko. A sharp, simple gesture, before pulling his gloves off with his teeth and flexing stiff fingers.

Neither man spoke. The mechanic nearest Veikko opened his mouth to ask something, then thought better of it. *Good man. I just want to be inside my head right now.*

Veikko strode across the packed snow toward the command tent. His boots punched through the icy crust with each step. The brittle surface gave way under his weight, and crunching loudly in the otherwise silent airfield. Every step felt heavy, the brittle wind dragging at his coat and flight gear, tugging him back toward the flight line. He ignored it. His path was straight, steady, and without hesitation, the same way he had flown.

Captain Nieminen was already outside, pipe in one hand, eyes locked on the flight line. He said nothing as Veikko approached, only jerked his chin toward the tent flap.

Inside, a map was already unrolled on the table, markers scattered across the surface like spilled ammunition. Veikko stood at attention. "Report," Nieminen said without looking up.

"Bait executed," Veikko said. "Wolfpack engaged. Formation shattered."

Nieminen looked up then, one eyebrow lifting slightly. "Leader?"

"Wounded. Escaped east under smoke. Reinforcements inbound prevented me from finishing him off."

For a moment, neither spoke. The only sound was the low hiss of the stove in the corner and the distant cough of another engine backfiring somewhere beyond the tents. Nieminen tapped the stem of his pipe against the table once. The impact created a dry, and deliberate sound. "Partial success then," he said finally.

Veikko said nothing. The word success felt hollow in his mouth. Victories were measured in wreckage, in men who didn't come back, and in enemies who no longer breathed the same air. The Wolfpack might have been scattered today, but their leader still lived. As long as he did, the threat remained. *This wasn't victory. It was a delay. A stay of execution. Nothing more.*

Veikko stepped back into the daylight. Immediately, the cold hit him. The frigid air felt raw and sharp against the sweat still cooling on his skin. The airfield buzzed with life in a way it hadn't all week. Mechanics shouted across the line. Ground crews slapped each other on the back. A few pilots clustered around the stove outside the mess tent, laughing too loud, mugs of steaming tea clenched in their hands.

Someone had already chalked a new tally mark on the board next to the dispersal hut, another bomber down, another fighter scratched off. The illusion of victory hung in the air like smoke. Veikko kept walking, the sounds washing over him without sinking in. *It hadn't been a clean victory or even been a real one. Chernyavin was still alive.*

Somewhere east of here, under the same frozen sky, the man was nursing his wounds, studying his failures, and planning his next move. Veikko pulled his scarf up higher against the wind. He didn't blame the others for celebrating.

They needed the lie. Needed the story that said today was different. That they had turned the tide, but Veikko knew better.

The Wolfpack wasn't dead. It was only wounded, and sometimes, a wounded wolf was more dangerous than one that had never been hurt at all. Pain sharpened instincts. Fear drove desperation, and desperation made killers reckless. Veikko knew better than to mistake today's broken formation for victory. They hadn't finished it. Far from it, they had only made it angry.

Captain Nieminen found him near the fuel depot. No salute or orders barked across the line. Just a low voice carried under the wind as Nieminen fell into step beside him.

"Walk with me," he said.

Veikko adjusted his stride automatically and unconsciously matched the captain's gait. A side effect from learning to march during his initial training that still lingered in the back of his mind years later. He followed Nieminen past the half-buried fuel drums and the skeletal remains of the maintenance tents. They skirted the edge of the motor pool. The noise of the celebrating crews fading behind them.

Only when they were beyond easy earshot did

Nieminen speak again. "Intelligence from Viipuri just came through," he said, voice low. "Soviet fighter activity's increasing along the northern sectors. Near Lake Suvanto."

Veikko's jaw tightened. It was too soon. Too organized for simple retaliation. "They're regrouping," Veikko said.

Nieminen nodded grimly. "Not just regrouping. They've shifted tactics by dispersing their flights. According to the reports, they are doing wide sweeps and not using mass formations."

"They're hunting singly. With their numbers, they can cover everywhere and sweep us from the skies," Veikko said, the realization sinking in fast. "If one of them makes a contact, it won't take long for reinforcements to arrive. Worse, they'll be impossible to anticipate as they converge from different directions piecemeal."

Nieminen lit his pipe, shielding the flame from the wind with his glove. He took two short draws before answering. "They're adapting, Lieutenant," he said, "or someone's teaching them to."

Neither man had to say the name aloud. Chernyavin. Veikko looked eastward, beyond the gray line of the horizon. *The Wolfpack wasn't dead. It was mutating. Worse, it seemed to be growing, and whatever came next would be worse.*

They walked a few more paces before Nieminen spoke again, his voice a little quieter now. "And your men?" he asked. "How did they hold up?"

Veikko considered before answering. He thought of Virtanen, grimacing but steady. Of Rautio, his voice tight but unbroken when the fight closed on them. And Kuusela, the ghost on his wing, silent, efficient, exactly where he needed to be.

"They flew well," Veikko said finally. "Tight under pressure. No panic. They followed orders."

Nieminen gave a slow nod, the kind that wasn't approval so much as acknowledgment. Experience speaking to experience. "And their nerves?" he pressed. "It's not the flying that breaks men. It's waiting for the next one."

Veikko exhaled slowly, watching his breath curl into the cold air. "They're rattled," he admitted. "Not broken. But if this drags out—" he left the rest unsaid.

Nieminen grunted. "It always drags out. The Red Airforce has the machines and the manpower to wait us out. They are relentless."

They paused near a half-dug snow trench where crates of spare parts sat half-buried under drifted snow. Tools lay scattered where mechanics had abandoned them in favor of more urgent repairs. Beyond the trench, the airfield stretched out in grim silence, the ground pitted and scarred by days of heavy landings and rushed takeoffs. The tents sagged against the rising wind, their canvas flapping like broken flags under a sullen, bruised sky that promised more snow before nightfall. Everything about the place spoke of exhaustion, patched over, but not healed.

"You'll keep them tight, Lieutenant," Nieminen said, tapping the side of his pipe with one gloved finger. "You see a crack forming, one man slipping. you ground him. No heroics. There is no place for pride. I don't want any losses because someone couldn't hack it."

"I will," Veikko said.

"Good," Nieminen said simply.

He started walking again, and Veikko fell back into step

beside him, both men silent now, both knowing it would only get harder from here. They parted without a word each heading in a different direction. Veikko toward the flight line and Nieminen back to the command tent.

Veikko arrived back at the flight line after sunset. The cold had deepened, turning the snow underfoot into a brittle crust that cracked and splintered with every step. The wind had picked up too. It tugged at the tie-downs on the grounded planes and rattled the empty fuel drums stacked along the dispersal line.

The Fokkers sat in a neat row, dark shapes hunkered under the growing gloom. Frost clung to their wings and struts, catching what little light was left and turning it into a dull, lifeless sheen. They looked less like machines now and more like beasts crouched in the snow, waiting, patient and still. Waiting to be summoned into the sky for the next fight. Like hunting dogs leashed to a post, silent but ready to tear free at the first crack of a whip.

Veikko moved to his own machine, trailing a gloved hand lightly along the fuselage. The skin of the plane was cold and rough under the frost. He checked the wing mounts, the gun ports, and the landing gear. It felt like a meeting of two lovers that knew each other well. Both familiar and intimate. They danced through a ritual that was both spiritual and necessary.

He wasn't looking for damage but for reassurance. That when the next call came, the machine would answer him without hesitation. A pilot had to have confidence in his plane.

Behind him, the last of the ground crews packed up for the night. He caught a snippet of a lewd joke one of the men shared. Their laughter seemed faint under the rising howl of the wind.

Veikko stayed a little longer, running a thumb over the worn edge of the fuselage near the engine cowling. The paint had peeled away there, down to the bare cold steel beneath. *The same way this damn war would strip us all if it lasted long enough.*

He stepped back finally, the field empty around him except for the whisper of canvas and the brittle crunch of his own boots. The wolf hadn't died today. It had simply retreated into the dark. Tonight, it lurked in its den, licking its wounds. Tomorrow it would emerge, ready for the next hunt.

Veikko stood alone on the flight line, his silhouette dark against the deeper black of the night. The wind had died to a whisper, leaving the airfield wrapped in an unnatural silence. Frost crackled beneath his boots as he took a final look at the Fokkers—ghostly shapes under their canvas shrouds.

The sound of footsteps broke the stillness. Captain Nieminen approached. His pipe was unlit but still clenched between his teeth. He stopped beside Veikko, saying nothing for a long moment as they both stared at the grounded planes.

"You should be getting some rest," Nieminen said finally, his voice low enough that it barely disturbed the silence.

Veikko exhaled, his breath forming a pale cloud that dissipated into the darkness. "Not yet."

Nieminen pulled his pipe from his mouth and tapped it against his palm. "I saw your logbook. You've been flying more sorties than anyone else in the squadron."

"Someone has to."

"Someone doesn't have to be you every time." Nieminen's voice carried no reproach, just the quiet observation of a commander who'd seen too many men push themselves past breaking.

Veikko turned slightly. "You didn't come out here to count my flight hours."

Nieminen gave a curt nod, acknowledging the directness. "I came to ask you something I should have asked earlier. How are you holding up, knowing it's him out there?"

The question hung in the frigid air between them. Veikko's jaw tightened. For a heartbeat, he considered deflection, but there was no point. Nieminen knew too much.

"Two years," Veikko said finally. "Two years since he shot me down over Valencia. I spent six weeks in a hospital bed with a broken shoulder and shattered pride, watching other pilots die while I couldn't even climb into a cockpit."

Nieminen listened silently.

"He circled my wreckage," Veikko continued, the words coming faster now. "Just watching me. It was eerie. Strangely, he didn't fire another burst or go for the kill. Just observed, like I was some kind of specimen. Like my death wasn't even worth his attention."

He turned his face away, focusing on the distant tree line. "Every time I close my eyes, I can still see him through that canopy, watching me spiral down. I couldn't even die with dignity."

"And now you've found him again," Nieminen said.

"Or he's found us." Veikko's hand clenched at his side. "I damaged his plane today. Made him bleed, but it wasn't enough."

"It's not about enough. It's about surviving."

Veikko shook his head. "Not with him. Not with Chernyavin."

Nieminen studied Veikko's profile in the darkness. "You're putting a lot on your shoulders. This trap you're setting it carries risk."

"Every flight carries risk."

"Not the same risk. You're asking men to fly as bait."

The words struck like a physical blow. Veikko had spent days avoiding that very thought. "They're volunteers," he said finally.

"That doesn't make them expendable."

"You think I don't know that?" Veikko's voice hardened. "You think I don't see their faces every time I close my eyes? Virtanen, Halme, all of them."

He turned to face Nieminen directly. "I grew up in Viipuri. My grandfather's house stood five streets from the cathedral. There's nothing left of it now but ash and broken timber. When I flew over yesterday, I couldn't even find the street."

Nieminen nodded slowly. "I didn't know."

"Three generations of my family lived there. My father taught mathematics at the school. He used to take me flying on Sundays in an old Thulin he'd restored. Said the sky was where numbers made sense." Veikko's voice grew quieter. "He died last year. I'm glad he didn't get to see what they did to his city."

The captain was silent for a moment. "This isn't just about Chernyavin for you, then."

"Nothing is just about one thing anymore." Veikko stared up at the stars, faint pinpricks through the thin cloud cover. "But I know what you're asking. You want to know if I'm too focused on settling a score."

"Are you?"

Veikko considered the question with the same clinical precision he applied to flight paths and fuel calculations.

"If Chernyavin were just another Soviet pilot, he'd still need to be shot down," he said finally. "He's training others and creating doctrine. Every day he flies is another day his wolves get stronger."

"That's tactically sound," Nieminen said, "but it doesn't answer my question."

The silence stretched between them. When Veikko spoke again, his voice was barely audible. "I don't know if I can beat him." The admission felt like tearing open a wound. "Not in a straight fight. He flies like the aircraft is a part of him. Like he was born with wings instead of arms."

Nieminen nodded. "That's why you're setting the trap."

"It's the only way," Veikko's jaw set in a hard line, "but even then, I'm not sure."

"None of us are sure of anything anymore." Nieminen replaced his pipe, though he still didn't light it. "Just be certain of this: your worth isn't measured by whether you kill Chernyavin. It's measured by how many of our boys make it home because of what you teach them."

Veikko didn't respond immediately. The statement cut against everything, driving him forward.

"Get some rest, Lieutenant," Nieminen said finally. "Tomorrow will demand everything you have."

The captain turned to leave, then paused. "And Veikko, I've seen men consumed by vengeance before. They rarely survive it, and they rarely help others survive either."

With that, he was gone, boots crunching across the hard-packed snow toward the command tent.

Veikko remained alone, his thoughts circling like aircraft in a holding pattern, searching for a clear approach to the truth. After a long moment, he turned away from the flight line and headed toward the pilot's quarters.

The wolf hadn't died today. It had simply retreated into the dark. Tonight, it lurked in its den, licking its wounds. Tomorrow it would emerge, ready for the next hunt.

Chapter 8

Forward Airfield, Outside Viipuri

December 2, 1939

The cold had further deepened overnight. It settled into the ground and the bones of the men who moved across the airfield stiffly. A heavy mist clung low over the snow, blurring the outlines of the tents and grounded planes. It was the kind of morning that swallowed sound, where even boot steps seemed muffled under the brittle crust of ice.

Veikko stood outside the mess tent, a tin mug of black coffee cooling fast in his gloved hands. The bitter smell cut through the damp air, but the heat didn't reach him. Nothing did anymore.

Around him, the camp moved with a kind of tired efficiency. No shouting. No jokes. Just work: the endless cycle of repairs, refueling, rearming. Preparing for the next call to scramble that might come or might not. Hope and dread tied together so tightly that neither feeling had any strength left.

A runner came out of the command tent. He slipped a little on the frozen ground as he sprinted toward the flight line. His face was pinched and tight, his breath ghosting behind him in ragged streams.

Veikko watched him go without moving. He already knew. Captain Nieminen stepped out of the tent a moment later, tugging on his gloves with sharp, irritated jerks. His pipe was clamped between his teeth, but it wasn't lit.

Their eyes met across the yard. Nieminen didn't have to say it aloud. Another patrol was missing. No radio call or contact. Just gone.

The mist thickened as the sun struggled to climb above the treetops, turning the world into a flat, silver blur. It wasn't just the weather closing in. It was the war itself.

Forward Command Tent – Thirty Minutes Later

The canvas walls sagged inward under the weight of the mist. The single stove in the corner coughed fitfully. It did little to push back the damp cold that seeped through every seam.

Lieutenant Veikko Niemi stood near the back of the tent. His helmet was tucked under one arm, and his eyes were steady as the other squad leaders shuffled in. Their boots knocked clumps of frozen snow from their soles, scattering grit and ice across the floorboards. Every breath turned white in the bitter air, curling up toward the sagging canvas roof.

Captain Nieminen was already at the map table, pipe in hand, but still unlit. His face was drawn tighter than usual. He waited until the last man was through the flap before speaking.

"We lost the Gray Three Patrol this morning," he said without preamble. His voice was flat. Stripped of everything but fact.

A low murmur ran through the tent. "Last contact was thirty minutes after takeoff," Nieminen continued. "No distress call or visual sightings. Nothing since."

He stabbed the map with the end of his pipe, marking a thin strip of white that snaked through the frozen forests north of Lake Suvanto. "They were operating here. Same sector we discussed yesterday. Spread thin and the visibility was garbage."

Veikko listened without blinking. They weren't flying patrols anymore. They were lambs waiting for the wolf-pack to slaughter them and the wolves had learned how to use the fog to their advantage.

Nieminen straightened and drew a slow breath through his nose, as if weighing every word. "Effective immediately," he said. "Patrols will extend further east and north. Solo or two-ship elements only. We don't have the planes to support larger groups.

A ripple of protest rose. A low curse came from the Lapland boys, and a muttered argument from the 26th Squadron. Nieminen cut it off with a raised hand. "You don't like it?" he said, voice rough. "Write a letter to headquarters. Maybe they'll send more planes. Until then, we fly what we have. Where we must."

He turned his gaze across the room, landing hard on each man. "To stay alive, you must be flexible. Radio silence unless engaged. If you make contact, you pull them west away from their bases and back into sectors we control. You don't play hero east of Suvanto. You get caught out there, you're dead."

He tapped the map again. "Questions?"

No one answered. The silence settled heavily over the room. It was thicker than the smoke that hung in the stale air. Every man in the tent knew the truth even if no one spoke it aloud. There were no good questions left to ask. No clever tactics that could change what was coming. They would fly, and some would not return. It wasn't courage anymore. It was inevitability.

The Fokker sat waiting at the edge of the hard pack. Its canvas covers already peeled back and folded stiffly against the ground. Frost steamed from the exhaust ports where the mechanics had preheated the engine.

Thin wisps of vapor curled up into the gray mist like smoke from a dying fire. Ice clung stubbornly to the wing struts and around the landing gear, refusing to yield even to the engine's rough warmth. The plane looked less like a machine now and more like a living thing, something restless, and eager to tear into the sky again, even if it didn't return.

Veikko approached alone. No one called out or wished him luck. Everyone on the flight line understood that certain flights didn't merit words. He moved like a man performing a ritual. Each step deliberate and exact.

He pulled the sheepskin-lined flight helmet down over his ears, fastened the chin strap. Tightened his scarf once, then again, until it bit into the sides of his neck. He checked his gloves and the pistol at his side. Not because he thought he would need it, but because rituals mattered.

At the wing root, a ground crewman waited with the logbook tucked under one arm.
Sergeant Aleksi Mikkola, an old mechanic with deep lines and leathery skin from years spent on the flight line scowled as Veikko approached. *Mikkola seems to have a permanent scowl on his face. I don't think I've ever seen him smile.* His thought ended as he realized, *I guess I don't smile much either.*

Mikkola didn't salute. He never did. He just held out the book and said, "Nothing new broken. Yet. . ."

Veikko took it and scrawled his name with a half-frozen pencil. "Good work getting her ready," he said.

Mikkola snorted. "I keep fixing 'em. You lot keep trying to tear 'em apart."

He moved to the wing and ran a thick, gloved hand along the seam near the fuel intake. His movements were rough but careful, the way a man might check the hooves of an old horse he still respected. "Full tanks," Mikkola grunted. "Guns tight. If you break this one, try to bring back enough pieces this time so I can stitch it together again. Laaksonen over in supply had to trade a burlap sack and a night with his wife to get this new gun. "

Veikko gave a thin smile, more out of habit than humor. "I'll see what I can do." He paused for a moment, then asked, "Why did the seller want a sack?"

Mikkola snorted. "To put over her head. She's half Russian and plenty ugly."

Veikko chuckled. Mikkola stepped back, arms folded across his chest. "Just bring yourself back, Lieutenant.

Planes I can fix. . ."

For a second, neither man said anything. Then Veikko climbed into the cockpit without another word. The moment he set his right foot on the bottom rung of the ladder, the conversation faded away as his thoughts shifted to the mission.

He climbed up into the cockpit as the ladder groaned under his weight. The seat was cold and stiff, the leather biting through even the thick layers of his flight suit. He settled in, strapping himself down, every buckle familiar under his fingers.

The flight controls were stiff, but responsive. He ran through the quick checks almost by feel: Throttle loose. Rudder responsive. Primer pump firm and the weapons safeties on.

Outside, the mist thickened across the field. It swallowed the far tents, the trees, and the world beyond. When he keyed the ignition, the Fokker's engine coughed twice, then roared to life, a deep, ragged sound that rattled through the canopy and into his bones.

He sat there for a moment, hand on the throttle, letting the vibrations settle into his spine. No fear or anger. Only the cold certainty that he would meet whatever waited out there with open eyes.

Veikko pushed the throttle forward. The Fokker shuddered against the tie-downs. Mikkola released them, and another maintainer yanked the chocks clear. He taxied out onto the snow-packed strip, nose pointing east into the fog.

Above the Forests – Early Afternoon

Veikko eased the throttle forward, and the Fokker

lurched into a slow, stubborn crawl. The wheels crunched over the frozen hard pack, the thin snow kicking up in dusty sprays under the tires. The airframe vibrated under him, a low and steady tremor that settled into his legs and spine.

Ahead, the strip stretched out in a pale, uneven line, flanked by shadowed banks of plowed snow. The edges had hardened into rough, broken walls. Lanterns shielded under heavy canvas hoods threw small, flickering pools of yellow light onto the track, but beyond that, the mist swallowed everything.

The rudder pedals were stiff in the cold, and Veikko worked them carefully, steering with slow, deliberate taps. The wind tugged at the wings, trying to tip him sideways. He fought it automatically, without thought, keeping the nose aligned into the faint headwind.

The ground crew watched from the sidelines. They were bundled in greatcoats, and their faces were hidden behind scarves and frost-crusted goggles. No waves or salutes. Just silent, hunched figures waiting to see if he'd come back.

Veikko reached the end of the strip. He kicked the rudder to swing the nose into the wind and braked gently. The Fokker shuddered to a halt.

He ran through the final checks, quickly set the trim to neutral, and checked the oil pressure which was steady. His gloved hand tightened around the stick, feeling the plane straining, eager to be unleashed. A thin gust scoured the strip, rattling the fuselage. He pushed the throttle forward.

With a howl of the engine against the cold, the Fokker surged into motion, its wheels hammering the frozen ruts. The tail lifted first, then the nose, and the whole machine clawed its way off the ground. The wheels lifted clean from the snowpack with a soft jolt.

The Fokker climbed into the mist almost immediately, swallowed whole by the low ceiling before he'd cleared the end of the strip. The world below vanished in a second. There was no horizon, or landmarks, only the dim, uniform gray of the overcast.

Veikko eased back on the stick, leveling off at a thousand meters. The engine thrummed steadily. The sound it created was low, rough music that filled the cockpit and wrapped around him like a second heartbeat.

He flew by instruments now. His altimeter was steady, and the compass drifting against the crosswinds. The turn-and-bank indicator twitched with every small adjustment. The world outside the windscreen was nothing but a cold, shifting void.

He keyed the radio once, a short pulse to confirm he was airborne. No chatter or acknowledgments. Only static. The protocol was silence unless engaged.

The field shrank behind him. Ahead stretched the endless white expanse of the eastern forests, blurred and featureless under the low clouds. *Alone. Exactly as planned.*

He flew on, scanning the mist ahead for any sign of movement, and somewhere beyond that veil, he knew something was already watching him.

The mist thickened as Veikko pressed eastward. Visibility tightened to little more than the length of a football field. The ground below was lost under the cloud cover. Only the pale ghost of his instruments and the muted thrum of the engine tied him to anything real.

He kept his eyes moving, left, right, scanning high and

low. Minutes dragged by, slow and heavy. *Nothing.*

Only the endless gray, the hiss of wind across the canopy, and the rhythmic vibration of the frame. Veikko banked slightly north. He felt the shift of the crosswind bite into his wingtip and adjusted without thinking. Small corrections he did on instinct without thinking about it.

He was just beginning to relax. Something flickered at the edge of his vision, as he began to think he might have another empty patrol to report. He snapped his head left.

A shadow moved, fast, low, and wrong. Too fast for a bird. Too low for mist. Too sharp to be imagination. It disappeared almost immediately into the fog.

Veikko tightened his grip on the stick. No radio traffic or warning. *Whatever it was, it hadn't wanted to be seen.*

His heartbeat increased its pace, not a surge of fear, but the tight, hot quickening of a hunter spotting the barest ripple in the underbrush. He keyed the radio twice, two short clicks, silent code to base: *possible contact, no engagement yet.*

Nothing came back. Just static. He eased the throttle forward slightly, building speed. The mist shifted ahead of him, curling and parting in strange, broken shapes.

Somewhere out there, in the cold silence, the Wolfpack had learned a new trick and they were waiting. The mist peeled back for a heartbeat. Veikko caught the shape, bigger this time. Sharper. *An I-16. Maybe two.*

Low and slow, almost invisible against the frozen forest that blurred beneath the fog cover. *They weren't moving fast or hunting. They were waiting. Bait.*

Veikko's stomach tightened. *It wasn't a mistake or an*

accident. This was a setup.

He rocked the Fokker into a shallow bank, angling slightly west, feigning ignorance. The Soviets didn't react. They kept flying low and lazy. Showing just enough to be seen.

Trying to lure him closer. He eased the throttle back, to buy himself some time. The clouds shifted again, another ripple, and this time he saw them. *Four shapes. Maybe five.*

Parked in the mist above him, holding altitude in a loose, layered wedge. *Not amateurs or a random patrol. Coordinated. Waiting for me to pounce on the bait so they could fall onto his back. The Wolfpack hadn't scattered after Chernyavin's wound. They had evolved.*

He keyed the mic once, a short and sharp click. *Confirmed multiple hostiles.*

Still no response. He was alone and the trap was already closing. Veikko gritted his teeth, the familiar pressure building behind his ribs, that cold, burning focus that came before every real fight. *I'm not running.* He smiled ruefully. *At least not yet.*

He pushed the throttle forward, feeling the engine roar through the frame. He angled lower, flattening his climb, staying unpredictable. *If they wanted a hunt, he'd give them one. On his terms.*

The bait moved first. One of the low-flying I-16s broke formation, angling upward in a slow, lazy climb. *Temptation laid bare.*

Veikko ignored it. He banked right, shallow and easy, keeping his speed up, showing no sign of biting. Above him, the real threat shifted. The high flight tightened their wedge, nose angles dropping ever so slightly. *They were getting ready to dive. Timing and coordinating it.*

Waiting for the moment when he would commit himself low, where he'd have no altitude left to maneuver, nowhere to run. Veikko grinned behind the mask. *Not today.*

He yanked the stick hard right, rolling into a tight turn and dropping the Fokker into a controlled dive. Not toward the bait, but away, cutting perpendicular across the Wolfpack's setup. The sky exploded. Three I-16s peeled out of the mist, diving after him, their engines snarling like a pack unleashed.

Tracer fire stitched the air around him wild at first, then tightening as they adjusted. Veikko hauled the Fokker into a break turn, the G-forces hammering into his chest, and the wings groaning under the strain. The mist blurred past the canopy, gray and shapeless.

He kept his turn tight, bleeding speed but staying unpredictable, forcing them to follow him through a tightening spiral instead of diving for a clean kill. The Soviets followed, but not perfectly.

The lead fighter kept up, but the second hesitated a fraction, and the third drifted too wide, losing angle. *Gaps. Tiny, but widening.* Veikko felt it in his bones. *They were good, but they were hungry. Pressing too hard and making mistakes.*

He flattened the spiral into a low slashing dive, forcing the lead I-16 to commit or overshoot. The Soviet tried to follow and match him. Veikko cut throttle, tightened the turn until the Fokker's wings screamed in protest and the Soviet fighter flashed past his nose. *Too fast and shallow. He over committed.*

Veikko rolled out, throttled up, and latched onto his six. Gun sights settled. His thumb tensed on the trigger.

Veikko squeezed the trigger. The Brownings barked, and the recoil vibrated through the stick. Tracers slashed through the fogged air, cutting a tight line across the I-16's fuselage. The Soviet pilot reacted late.

Rounds punched through the Polikarpov's rear canopy, stitching the engine housing and wing root. Black smoke erupted instantly, trailing back in a thick, greasy ribbon. The I-16 bucked violently, trying to climb away, but the damage was done.

The fighter lurched upward in a desperate, half-hearted climb, then stalled.
It tipped sideways like a stone dropped from a sling, nose dipping into a slow, doomed spiral. Veikko throttled back instinctively, watching for a chute, for any sign of survival. *Nothing.*

Just the crippled fighter spinning into the mist, swallowed whole by the endless white. *One down, but no time to watch it die.*

The second and third Soviet fighters were already angling back onto his tail, adjusting for the kill. Veikko rolled hard left, diving low, back toward the cloud bank. Tracer fire licked past his canopy, savage and close.

He fought the Fokker through the turbulence, the frame rattling as he punched into a lower layer of mist. Vision dropped to a handful of meters. He was forced to fly on instinct through the murky grayness.

He banked blindly, rolling left, then hard right. Then kicked the rudder to throw off their aim. Shots cut past him again, wide this time, spraying empty air.

He broke through the bottom of the cloud layer and for one heartbeat, the world snapped into view. Frozen rivers below. Thick pine forests dusted with ice and three more fighters rising out of the fog ahead.

Not the ones he'd been fighting. New ones. Fresh, that had been waiting.

The realization hit Veikko like a blow to the gut. They hadn't just sent bait and a strike team. They had sent two echelons, one to drive him low, and the other to cut off the escape. *A hammer and anvil.* He grinned. *Well maybe in their case a hammer and sickle.*

He didn't hesitate. Throttle wide open, he yanked the stick back, forcing the Fokker into a brutal high-G barrel roll. His body slammed into the seat harness, the blood draining from his head as the wings screamed under the strain.

Tracers ripped the air where he had been a second before. No formation or elegant turns. Just survival.

He leveled out facing west, back toward Finnish lines. He was deep into Soviet-controlled airspace now, and the Wolfpack was closing from all sides. The fresh fighters swung into a wide pincer. Two angled high, trying to box him from above, another low and fast, cutting off the ground escape.

A lesser pilot would have climbed. Tried to punch upward through them.
Predictable. Easy to bracket and kill. Veikko dropped lower instead, skimming the treetops, using the mist and the fractured light of the frozen rivers to mask his movement.

The altimeter spun down. One hundred meters. Then seventy-five.

The tree line blurred past beneath his wings, white and green flashing in dizzying patterns. The Fokker bucked and shivered in the denser air, but Veikko kept the nose down, threading between the rising banks of fog. Above him, the Wolfpack circled, hesitant now, uncertain whether to commit fully or risk collision with the terrain.

He had a sliver of time. A narrow crack between the jaws closing around him. He jammed the rudder hard left, rolled inverted, and dropped under a frozen ridge line, vanishing into the thicker mist beyond.

No horizon, ground, or sky. Only instinct and a burning desire to survive. He drew comfort from the pulse of the machine under his hands, and the knowledge that if he guessed wrong once, he would die without ever seeing the shot that killed him.

Veikko held his breath and flew blind. The mist closed over him like a coffin, blinding, smothering. The only reference was the trembling needles of his instruments and the raw vibration of the Fokker under his boots.

Behind him, engines snarled, closer now. At least one Soviet pilot had bitten. *Hungry, eager, and reckless.* He smiled. *Perfect.*

Veikko dipped lower, skimming the frozen river now, the black ice flashing past so close he could almost feel the cold bleeding up through the fuselage. He could hear the pursuing engine now, hammering in his wake, the angry whine of a plane pushed too hard, and low.

No time for a clean fight or room for a rolling duel. He would use the land and let the earth kill him. Veikko spotted it through a break in the mist, a rise of ice-blasted trees crowding close over a sharp bend in the river, their skeletal branches clawing out over the water. *No time for finesse.*

He pushed the stick forward, dropping even lower, and

hugging the riverbank as the trees loomed. Behind him, the Soviet tried to match the move. He glanced over his left shoulder and saw that the enemy plane was still following.

There was a flash of movement, a shadow too late to pull up, and then a dull, wet sound, like a hammer striking flesh. Veikko caught a glimpse of the I-16 as it clipped the treetops, shearing its left wing clean off. The Soviet fighter spun once, twice, and then disintegrated in a burst of white snow and shattered wood. *Gone.*

Veikko yanked the Fokker into a tight, banking turn. His engines screamed as he used the tree line to break contact before the others could re-acquire him. He didn't celebrate. There was no time. *The Wolfpack was still hunting, and he was still within reach of their teeth.*

The mist thickened again, choking off the broken world around him. Veikko leveled out just above the trees, wings shivering against the turbulent air. His breath rasped harshly inside the flight mask. The cold bit through the seams of his flight suit, gnawing at his hands and knees.

He angled west, pushing for the thinnest edge of the front lines, where friend and enemy blurred together in the snow. Behind him, faint at first, the snarl of engines rose again. *Not many, two, or maybe three. Still organized and hunting.*

He punched the throttle forward, forcing every ounce of speed out of the Fokker's battered frame. The vibrations deepened, settling into his bones as the nose trembled under the strain. The compass drifted and the altimeter twitched.

The world shrank to nothing but feel. The slight buffet of crosswinds, and the heavier gusts pushing down from above. He flew by instinct now; the terrain flickering past in broken flashes.

He risked a glance back. Two black shapes, vague in the fog, still tracking him. Tight and relentless, they pursued him. Not the wild conscripts used for bait but Wolfpack survivors. *The best of them.*

His muscles ached from constant tension. His fingers were going numb inside his gloves. The low fuel warning light flickered on the panel, faint and yellow in the gray gloom. *Not much longer.*

Ahead, the mist thinned for a heartbeat. The tree line broke. He caught a glimpse of frozen lakes and dark pine ridges. Terrain he recognized. *Finnish territory. Almost home.*

He tightened his grip on the stick, ignoring the fatigue grinding into his chest. He wasn't out yet. Not until he cleared the line. Not until the Wolfpack peeled off or bled out, trying to follow him. He gritted his teeth and flew harder, lower, faster, with every beat of his heart hammering one word into the freezing air: *Survive.*

The mist shredded around him as he burst into the open air. Below, frozen lakes stretched like broken mirrors across the landscape, their surfaces cracked and gleaming in the pale light. Pines knifed up in black ridges along the hills. *Finnish controlled territory. Barely.*

There was no time to climb. No time to wave a flag. The Wolfpack was still on him.

Bullets tore past his left wingtip, close enough that he felt the shock ripple through the frame. The nearest Soviet fighter dived lower, trying to cut him off before he could reach safety. Veikko shoved the stick forward and snapped the Fokker into a brutal dive toward the lakes. Ice and water flashed up at him at terrifying speed. The cold howled through the gaps in the fuselage.

He pulled up at the last second. His wheels brushed the frozen lake surface, and the undercarriage skimming frost in a spray of white shards. Behind him, the Soviet fighter tried to follow. *Too late. A mistake.*

The I-16's tail wheel clipped the edge of the frozen lake. The fighter pitched forward, slammed into the ice, and cartwheeled in a fountain of debris. *Gone.*

Veikko didn't watch it crash. He was already climbing. The last Soviet held back, hesitated, then broke off, banking away into the mist. No pursuit or shots. *The fight was over.*

Veikko leveled out just above the treetops, the Fokker groaning under the strain. His fuel gauge flickering on empty. The wind shrieked past the canopy. He throttled back to conserve what little power remained. His heart still hammering, and his body soaked in cold sweat inside his flight suit.

He didn't shout or grin. He was dumbfounded that he was still alive. Veikko just flew west, toward the base. *Alive! For now. . .*

Chapter 9

Forward Airfield, Outside Viipuri

December 2, 1939

The runway lights were little more than blurred ghosts in the mist when Veikko's Fokker finally staggered back onto the strip. His plane's engine was coughing like an old man too tired to keep breathing. He kept the nose high as long as he dared to bleed speed, while he tried to coax the battered machine down without tearing it apart.

The wheels hit hard, too hard, but the landing gear held with a tortured groan. The tail dropped, and the Fokker rattled down the frozen hard pack. Each jolt seemed to punch up through the frame into Veikko's spine.

He coasted to a stop near the dispersal line and killed the engine with a final, exhausted shove of the cutoff switch. The prop spun twice more, then wheezed into silence. The sudden silence roared in his ears.

For a moment, he simply sat there. His gloved hands were locked around the stick, and his chest heaved under the weight of a fight that wasn't over. The canvas flaps around the maintenance tents rustled. Shapes moved through the mist. Ground crew, mechanics, and medics, all trotted toward him. His mind focused on the crunching noise their heavy boots made in the brittle snow.

They didn't cheer or shout. Instead, they set about their duties with a quiet sense of urgency. One of the medics stepped onto the ladder. He was a short man with sharp eyes and frost crusted in the seams of his cap. His canvas bag thumped against his hip as he climbed the ladder to the cockpit.

"Any pain?" he asked, already checking Veikko's pupils with a small penlight.

Veikko blinked once at the brightness. "Nothing new."

"You hit your head?"
"No."
"Black out at any point?"
"No."

The medic's hands moved quickly, pressing along Veikko's ribs, checking for blood at the joints of his flight suit. "Breathing normal?"
"As normal as it gets."
"Sharpness in your chest?"
"No."
"Vision blurred?"
"Only from the mist and the last hour of hell."

The medic gave a soft grunt and leaned back. "You're coherent. Cold as death but functional. Pulse is high."
"I'm alive," Veikko said. "That's the part that matters."

The medic nodded once. "You'll feel the shakes in about ten minutes. Eat something before then."

"I'll think about it," Veikko muttered.

The medic grunted in acknowledgement and climbed down. He fumbled the harness loose and half-fell, half-climbed down the side of the fuselage. His legs buckled when he hit the ground, knees almost giving way before he caught himself on the wing strut.

"Lieutenant!" someone called, maybe Mikkola, maybe another mechanic, but Veikko waved them off.

"I'm fine," he rasped, though the words felt hollow in his throat. My legs are a bit stiff. They'll loosen up."

One of the ground crew caught his arm and steadied him as another man rushed to chock the wheels. Veikko didn't resist. His muscles felt hollowed out, trembling from cold and exhaustion, but his mind stayed sharp. Sharp enough to know he'd only outrun death by a heartbeat and that it was waiting for him again. Somewhere out there, just beyond the edge of the mist.

Forward Command Tent – Twenty Minutes Later

The stove inside the tent popped once, struggling against the cold. The walls sagged with moisture, and the canvas was darkened with condensation. Maps were pinned to every surface, creased, curling, marked with layers of pencil and grease.

Captain Nieminen didn't look up as Veikko stepped through the flap. He was bent over the field table, pipe clamped between his teeth, and his eyes fixed on a fresh sheet of radio intercepts.

Veikko stamped the snow from his boots, flexed his frozen fingers, and stepped closer.

"You made it," Nieminen said at last, voice low. Not a question but fact. Confirmation that he had come back.

Veikko nodded once. "Barely."

Nieminen pushed the report aside and looked up.

"What did you see?"

Veikko didn't answer right away. He stepped up to the table and pointed to a blank sector east of Suvanto. "They set bait," he said. "Two flights. One low. One layered high above it. Not conscripts. It was a well-timed ambush by disciplined professionals. I pray that the Red Air Force has few other pilots like these. If they do, this is going to be a really short war."

Nieminen's brow furrowed. "They waited for me to take the low path," Veikko continued. "Held the high one until I was committed. Then they dropped on me. They were perfectly coordinated, and their flying style was very precise."

"How many?"
"Six at least. I got two. Broke contact before the rest could box me in."

Nieminen leaned back, chewing on the stem of his pipe. "We've seen it in two other sectors today. Similar formations were described, but unlike you, they suffered losses. Yours is the first confirmation it's organized."

"It's more than organized," Veikko said. "It's doctrine."

He tapped the edge of the map with his gloved knuckle. "They're not hunting anymore. They're building a pattern. A system. Something they can use to teach their other pilots."

Nieminen didn't answer for a long moment. Outside, the wind clawed at the canvas, and the tent creaked like old bones. Finally, Nieminen said, "Then it's not a pack anymore."

Veikko met his eyes. "No. It's a school. If we don't put an end to Chernyavin, he will teach those bastards to sweep us from the sky."

Nieminen exhaled slowly through his teeth. "Then we're already behind," he said. "The moment we fly by the book, we're feeding them."

He turned toward the map again, jaw tightening as he studied the empty white between river lines and grid marks. "We've been sending out patrols like it's still November," he muttered. "Two-ship routines. Predictable altitudes and using the sector grids."

He jabbed a finger toward one of the red Xs marking a lost flight. "They're not chasing us. We're delivering men to their kill zones."

Veikko said nothing. The silence between them wasn't one of confusion, it was clarity. Ugly, necessary clarity.

Nieminen straightened, pipe still clenched between his teeth. "We'll need to stop flying by the book."

Veikko raised an eyebrow. "Meaning?"

"Meaning formation discipline takes a back seat. No more patrol grids. No standard altitudes. We scatter and rotate the lead constantly. Fly irregular on every flight."

Veikko nodded slowly. "Start flying like them."

"No," Nieminen said. "Start flying *worse*—unpredictably. Even Chernyavin can't out-think chaos."

He stepped to the other side of the map and pulled a

fresh sheet from the stack. The map displayed an open sector near the Isthmus where three flights had vanished in the last thirty-six hours. "We'll need volunteers. Solo or one-man bait. The only way to expose them is to let them strike and hope someone's watching when they do."

Veikko didn't speak. He didn't need to.

Nieminen's voice dropped. "We're not fighting the Red Air Force anymore. We're fighting *his* air force. His doctrine and his pilots."

Veikko looked down at the map, lines and marks, names of villages already burned or empty, and beneath it all, a war shifting under their feet.

"Then we'd better start unlearning everything we know," he said quietly.

Nieminen didn't disagree.

Pilot Tent – That Night

The canvas creaked with every gust of wind. Inside, the stove hissed and snapped, throwing a dull orange glow across the tent. Shadows danced along the sagging walls, stretching long over crates, boots, and sleeping gear.

Veikko stepped through the flap without a word. The warmth hit him first then the silence.

Virtanen looked up from the crate he was sitting on, a tin cup of tea cooling in his hands. Rautio lay on his bunk, one arm across his eyes. No one spoke. Kuusela sat nearest the stove, elbows on his knees, staring at the glowing coals like they might offer answers. He glanced at Veikko, met his eyes for a second, then looked away.

Virtanen cleared his throat softly and spoke without

looking up. "How'd it go, sir?"

Veikko sat for a moment, elbows on his knees, eyes fixed on the scuffed toes of his boots. "I came back. That's how it went."

Virtanen nodded slowly. "We heard the engine before we saw you. Mikkola said he'd already counted you out."

"He's not the only one."

Virtanen took a sip of his tea, winced at the bitterness. "How many were there?"

"Six. Maybe more." Veikko leaned back against the tent pole. The canvas was cold against his shoulders. "They weren't improvising. It was a setup. A layered ambush in two waves. Not amateurs."

Virtanen didn't speak for a while. Then, softly: "What do we do?"

Veikko looked at him then. Not as his superior officer but as a fellow pilot. Just a man talking to another man who would be flying tomorrow. "We fly different," he said. "We forget the patterns and stop being predictable."

Virtanen gave a humorless smile. "So we fly like drunks."

"No," Veikko said. "We fly like survivors."

He unstrapped his flight harness and hung it on a hook near the flap. His gloves followed, stiff with dried sweat. Then he crossed to his cot and sat down slowly, the weight of the day settling in all at once.

Rautio shifted on his cot, his arm dropping from over his eyes.

His voice came out flat, but not casual. "Sir, what did you see out there?"

Veikko didn't answer right away. The fire snapped. Someone coughed outside. He stared at the floor for a long moment before responding. "Everything," he said.

Coming to a decision, Veikko stood and walked to the end of his cot, where his footlocker lay. He opened it and pulled out a bottle of vodka and a shot glass. Slowly removing the vodka's cap, he attempted to steady his hand as he poured. He failed.

As Veikko poured his vodka, Rautio sat up slowly. His eyes were rimmed red from cold and fatigue, but they held steady. "Worse than the last time?"

Veikko downed his shot of vodka in one swallow and nodded. "They're not chasing us anymore. They're using positioning to set up kills."

Rautio looked down at his hands, rubbed his palms together like he was trying to warm something that wasn't cold. "They fly like ghosts," he muttered. "Guys are saying they don't talk. Don't break. Like they know how we'll move before we move."

Veikko's voice was low. "That's because someone taught them how and if we don't start changing, he's going to teach a lot more."

Rautio swallowed hard. "How do we fight that?"

Veikko didn't offer a slogan or a speech. Instead, he was honest. "Unpredictably and lots of speed," he said.

Rautio was quiet for a moment. Then he said, "I don't know if I've got it, sir," in a voice that wasn't quite a whisper.

Veikko looked at him, really looked. The bravado Rautio wore during briefings was gone. His shoulders were tight, his hands clenched in his lap. Not from cold but from something deeper.

"When the fight starts," Rautio continued, "my hands shake. Not bad. Not enough to miss a shot. But I feel it like I'm already behind before the first turn."

Veikko leaned forward, forearms resting on his knees. "They should shake."

Rautio blinked in surprise. "If they didn't," Veikko said, "I'd ground you myself. You're not supposed to be comfortable in this. You're supposed to survive it."

Veikko raised his right hand so that Rautio could see it. Rautio's eyes widened slightly as he watched a slight tremor in Veikko's hand.

Rautio gave a small nod. "How do I know when the shaking turns into freezing? When it's not just nerves but something that'll get me, or someone else, killed?"

Veikko didn't answer right away. He looked at the stove, at the dull glow in its belly. "When you find yourself watching instead of flying," he said finally, "that's when it's time to hand in your wings and walk."

Rautio took that in, then nodded once, slow and deliberate. "I'm not there yet," he said.

"No," Veikko agreed. "You're not."

Chapter 10

Forward Airfield, Outside Viipuri

December 3, 1939

The briefing tent was colder than the outside air. A single oil lamp hung from the ridgepole, its flame swaying slightly with every gust of wind. The heat from the stove hadn't reached the corners. Frost clung to the inner canvas like lace.

Veikko stood beside the field table, arms folded, while the pilots gathered. No chalkboard or printed patrol grids. Just a single hand-drawn map and a stack of flight cards filled out in pencil, already smudged.

The chatter was quiet. Everyone's eyes were sharper than yesterday. No one asked questions.

Nieminen stepped forward. His face looked even more carved than usual. "You all know what's changed," he said. "No set routes, box patrols, or formations. You fly wide, solo, or in loose pairs, and you never do the same thing twice. If you're thinking about doing something clever, assume Chernyavin thought of it first."

A few men glanced at each other at the mention of the name, but no one spoke it aloud. Veikko flipped through the flight cards and handed out assignments. When he reached Rautio, he held the card a second longer.

"Solo," Veikko said. "Eastern sector. You'll sweep low and slow, then break west along the lakes. Report anything."

Rautio took the card. His fingers didn't tremble, but his eyes flicked up to Veikko's for half a heartbeat. He met Veikko's gaze and drew comfort from the steely resolve in the older pilot's eyes.

"You'll do fine," Veikko said. It wasn't encouragement. Just a fact or perhaps a challenge to bolster the younger pilot's spirits.

Rautio nodded once. "I'll bring her home."

"See that you do."

Above the Eastern Lakes – Midday

The air was thin and glassy over the lakes, light bouncing off the ice in sharp, blinding angles. Rautio flew low. Too low, maybe but the wind against the belly of the Fokker was the only thing that kept his thoughts quiet.

The control stick trembled faintly under his gloves. Not from mechanical strain, just nerves cycling through the airframe like static. The new doctrine left him alone. Truly alone.

No wingman or route. Just a patch of sky and a list of kill zones he wasn't supposed to enter but might drift into anyway. He passed a tree line that looked familiar, then banked left, just to prove to himself he could still make decisions.

The Fokker obeyed smoothly, with no hesitation. Rautio exhaled and eased off the throttle slightly. "Eyes sharp," he muttered to himself.

Snow, pine trees, and frozen lakes stretched out before him. He saw a distant plume of smoke. *Probably from some half-dead farmhouse, maybe a truck burning miles off,* he thought. *No fighters or movement. At least not yet.*

He scanned the cloud layer above him, then dropped a little lower, hugging the edge of the mist. The ground flickered in and out beneath him ice, forest, and white nothingness stretched out before him.

He hadn't realized his hands were tightening on the stick until he heard the leather creak. He loosened his grip. "Breathe, dammit."

The headset crackled softly. Nothing intelligible, just the static of an empty net. He checked his fuel. *Still good. Altitude: steady.*

His instinct commanded him to turn soon. The part of him that remembered Veikko's words said: *not yet.*

He stayed low, tracing the curve of the lake. Somewhere out here, the wolves would be circling, but maybe, just maybe, they hadn't found him first.

He spotted it on the far side of the lake. *Not a plane.*

Just a shimmer in the clouds too smooth, too deliberate, like something trying not to move but failing. His fingers twitched over the stick. Nothing in the clouds now. Just that blur in his gut, that sense Veikko had warned them about: the one that tightened just before the sky broke open.

Rautio kept flying and tightened his turn. *Don't climb. Just keep it going nice and steady.*

Another flicker, this one is both lower and faster. A shadow sliding along the treetops, hugging the mist. *Something isn't right.*

He rolled right, gently. Gradually enough to not draw attention. "Not yet," he whispered.

He adjusted the trim and let the Fokker drift slightly west. He counted to five and then the world exploded.

The I-16 dropped from the cloud bank like a thrown axe. Tracer fire ripped through the space Rautio had just occupied. The tracers were red-orange slashes that sliced through the mist and vanished into the white beyond.

He yanked the stick hard left as his instincts took over. The Fokker rolled into a banking dive, skimming the lake's frozen edge as the bullets chased his tail. The headset exploded with static. Another burst cracked past his canopy close enough that glass spider-webbed across the corner of the windscreen. *That was too close.*

He jerked the throttle wide open, heart hammering. The nose dipped further as he dove for the forest line. Another Soviet fighter burst from the clouds above, joining the first. The trap hadn't been hasty; it had been patient. *Two predators. They'd waited for the perfect* mistake.

Rautio's hands trembled. Not badly but enough. The Fokker wobbled as he pulled up from the dive, and his wingtip scraped a low draft of fog too thick to see through.

The plane jolted, slight, but jarring. *Don't freeze, fly you fool.*

He steadied the stick. Eyes snapped to the instruments, altimeter, compass, throttle. His breath hissed through clenched teeth. The second I-16 angled for a high pass, trying to box him in. The first was already swinging around for the kill. He realized they were faster and more disciplined than him. *The Wolfpack.*

Rautio didn't climb. He dropped again, lower than he should've, cutting across a bend in the river like a man riding the edge of a blade. Snow kicked up behind him in ghost trails.

Tracer fire burst wide over his canopy. He banked hard into a left-side slip, rolled halfway, and popped out of the mist behind a thin tree line barely avoiding a full stall. His gloves were slick now, sweat pooling despite the cold, but he wasn't frozen. *Not yet.*

The Fokker bucked as he leveled out, trees flickering past below like teeth on a saw. The two I-16s adjusted fast, curling above him, tightening their formation. They didn't rush. They flew like they knew time was on their side.

Rautio's breath came in short bursts now, fogging the inside of his mask. His jaw clenched so tight it made his temples ache. Another burst of tracers slashed overhead, cutting the mist open in jagged flashes. They were herding him, pushing him west, but not quite letting him go. *One wrong roll, early climb, or moment of hesitation and I'm finished.*

He spotted a break ahead, a narrow defile in the forest, barely wider than a village road, the edges steep with snow-covered rock. *I can try.*

It was suicide if he misjudged the angle, but he couldn't run forever. He banked right and dropped low again. He pointed the Fokker's nose down, and the engine screamed as he committed. The trees closed around him in like walls.

The defile swallowed him. Behind him, one of the I-16s hesitated, then followed. *Only one.* Rautio's eyes narrowed. *Good.*

He waited until the trees forced the angle tighter, then slammed the stick left and kicked the rudder into a snap turn. The Fokker flipped sideways, rolled over the ridge wall, and came out the other side, dragging vapor and speed. He pulled up fast and felt the Gs press hard into his spine.

The Soviet behind him wasn't so lucky. Rautio caught the flash, a wing clipping rock, then a smear of metal and flame across the ridge. *One down.*

The other I-16 peeled off and vanished into the mist. Whether it had run or repositioned, Rautio didn't know and didn't care. He punched the throttle. *Time to go home.*

Forward Airfield – One Hour Later

The Fokker came in low and fast, skidding along the snow-packed strip with one wing dipped just a little too far. The tires bounced twice before catching. A groan echoed from the frame. Snow kicked up in a sharp arc as the plane finally slowed.

By the time Rautio rolled to a stop, the ground crew was already moving. They didn't cheer. They didn't wave. He was just another survivor, clawing his way back from the edge.

Rautio climbed down stiffly, hands shaking as he unbuckled his straps. His knees buckled when his boots hit the ground, but he caught himself on the wing before anyone noticed. Someone approached Mikkola, maybe or one of the younger crew. He wasn't sure. He waved them off. He didn't want warmth or questions. Not yet.

He walked alone across the hard pack. As he walked, his breath rose in ragged plumes. His scarf was half-untied, one glove hanging loose from his wrist. He didn't remember unfastening it. The pilot's tent was quiet when he stepped inside.

The stove popped. The air was thick with the sour smell of wool, smoke, and cold tea. Veikko was seated near the back, scribbling into a small, dog-eared logbook. He looked up. Their eyes met.

Rautio didn't speak. He just stood there for a moment as his shoulders sagged under a weight he hadn't had before. Veikko studied him, really studied him, then nodded once.

"You flew," he said. "That's what matters."

Rautio swallowed. "One of them crashed."

Veikko's pen stopped moving. "Because of you?"

Rautio hesitated. Then nodded. "Yes."

"Then it counts as your first kill," Veikko said. "Now do it again tomorrow."

Rautio blinked. Then, slowly, sat down on the edge of his bunk. No one said anything more. Something had shifted, and not just in the air.

Chapter 11

Forward Airfield, Outside Viipuri

December 4, 1939

They didn't fly in formation anymore. Instead, they scattered like seeds in the wind, loose and unpredictable. Each man was alone in the sky with only instinct and thin luck to guide him. There were no more tight turns, no synchronized climbs, no safety in numbers. Just empty air and the knowledge that the Soviets had learned their habits and were sharpening their claws against them. The Finns flew wide now, erratic, jagged across the map, and prayed that the wind blew crueler on the Russians than it did on them.

Dawn hadn't broken yet, but the flight line was already awake. Engines coughed against the cold. Ground crews moved like ghosts, shoulders hunched, speech low. Lanterns swayed from poles driven into the snowbanks, their yellow light throwing long shadows over canvas, crates, and hunched figures fastening belts and checking oil lines.

Rautio stood near his assigned Fokker, helmet under

one arm, scarf wrapped tight around his throat. His eyes were darker than they'd been yesterday. Less glass and more stone.

Kuusela approached from the shadow of the fuel truck, gloves already smudged with frost and grease. "You check your flaps?" he asked without greeting.

Rautio nodded. "Twice."

Kuusela jerked his chin toward the mist just beyond the edge of the dispersal line. "Low band's thicker today. You'll lose the horizon sooner."

"I know."

Kuusela stepped closer, voice low. "Then don't chase ghosts into it. Stay fast and break early. Let them commit first."

Rautio didn't answer right away. Then: "One of them chased me yesterday. He's not flying today."

Kuusela gave a short nod, almost approval. "Doesn't mean the next one won't be better." He turned to leave, then paused. "Don't forget, throttle gives you seconds, not distance. The terrain gives you space. Use it."

Rautio adjusted his gloves. "Understood."

Kuusela walked away without saying another word. Rautio watched him go, then turned back to his Fokker. He laid one hand on the wing like he had the night before. The metal was cold through the glove, but steady.

Somewhere behind him, a siren wailed once. Not an alarm. Just a scramble test. Still, every man turned and looked up.

Forward Command Tent – Shortly After Dawn

The canvas flap snapped once behind Veikko as he stepped into the tent. The cold followed him in, curling low around his boots. Captain Nieminen stood alone at the map table, the kerosene lamp burning low beside him. His pipe was clamped between his teeth, unlit.

He didn't look up. "There's a man from intelligence sitting in a crate on the edge of the runway," he said. "Looks like he dressed for a dinner party, not a war zone."

Veikko frowned. "Another liaison?"

"Something like that," Nieminen said. "He needs a ride to a signals post on an island west of the Isthmus. Command says it's urgent."

"I have a patrol window in less than two hours."

"You do," Nieminen agreed. "And you'll still have it. Take him and land on the ice next to the island. Don't come to a stop. Maybe slow down just enough that he won't die when you kick him out of the plane. Then come back fast."

Veikko stepped closer to the map, eyes scanning the sector east of the front line. A thin curve of frozen river that joined several lakes then the shore. A name he didn't recognize penciled beside a makeshift airstrip on the ice next to an island hardly larger than a rock.

He tapped the edge of the paper. "This post even operational?"

Nieminen finally looked at him. "They say it is. And command wants ears closer to the front. Too many of our patrols are vanishing into fog, and HQ's convinced we're missing intercept chatter."

"And they think one man with a suitcase can change that?"

"They think we're overreacting," Nieminen said, voice flat. "This is their way of reminding us who draws the map lines."

Veikko's mouth pulled into a tight line. "I'll take him."

"Good. He's your cargo now."

Veikko turned to leave. Nieminen's voice followed him. "Try not to show him what the war actually looks like."

Veikko didn't answer.

Above the Isthmus – Midmorning

The Fokker flew light. No external ammo cans, extra fuel or wingman.

Veikko kept it low and steady, the engine throttled back just enough to ride the smoother air above the treetops. The sky was dull gray, and the sun was buried somewhere behind a ceiling of dirty clouds. The air shimmered with ground haze and shallow bands of mist curling off the snowbound lakes.

Behind him, stuffed into the rear observer's seat with a suitcase crammed under his knees, the intelligence officer hadn't spoken in ten minutes. Veikko preferred it that way.

The man had introduced himself as Lehto, no rank or unit. Just a coat that looked too thin and boots that hadn't seen a day of frost. He gripped the cockpit rails like a man holding a subway pole.

After a while, Lehto leaned closer and shouted over the engine noise. "Much further?"

Veikko didn't answer. He just tapped two fingers against the side of the canopy frame, *nearly there*—and kept flying.

They passed over a frozen river. A burned-out truck sat jackknifed on the southern bank, its frame blackened and skeletal. Lehto didn't point. Didn't react. *Maybe he wasn't new to this after all.*

Veikko scanned the horizon, eyes constantly moving. His compass was steady and altitude was holding. Then he saw it.

Faint, west-southwest, just at the edge of the cloud cover. *A flicker or a formation?* He continued to peer intently and soon realized, *They're not fighters. Too wide and slow.* He tried squinting to make the dots out. *Twin-engine shadows crawling through the haze. Bombers.*

Veikko squinted again. *They weren't heading west toward the lines. They were angling northwest, toward the airfield. His airfield.*

He tapped the altimeter once. *No error. They were flying low. Too low for recon. This was a strike group.*

He keyed his mic, transmitting a short burst on the encrypted frequency. Then again. No response. Too far, or the Soviets were jamming the band.

Lehto leaned forward. "Problem?"

"Stay quiet," Veikko muttered. "Hold tight."

He banked the Fokker slightly and angled the nose homeward. His fingers tightened on the stick. The airfield was about to burn.

Forward Airfield – Ten Minutes Later

The klaxon began as a long, low groan, half warning, half question. Men looked up from fuel drums and ammo crates. Someone shouted from the comms tent, but the wind swallowed the words. A pair of mechanics froze in the middle of reattaching a cowling. Others ran, ducking instinctively, though nothing had struck yet.

Then the first bombs hit. The sound wasn't a crack or a boom. It was a deep, blunt *whomp* that seemed to come from under the earth itself.

The frozen ground jolted. Flames blossomed near the southern dispersal line, one of the fuel trucks going up like a kicked lantern. A geyser of smoke and fire curled upward, fast and filthy. More followed.

The sky filled with the high whine of diving engines. Dark shapes dropped out of the mist like knives. Soviet SB-2 bombers. Flying low and fast, they went unchallenged.

Rautio was already running, scarf trailing behind him, with his helmet half-fastened. He shoved past a crewman as another explosion staggered the row of grounded Fokkers. The impact flipped one clean over.

He didn't look back. Kuusela was already in motion, his boots hammering across the snow as he yanked a tarp off his fighter. "Start the damn trolley!" he roared, but the engine cart was overturned and burning ten meters away.

A shockwave slammed through the camp, punching the frozen air like a hammer against glass. Tents bowed and snapped, their canvas skins tearing open under the force. Snow and dirt erupted like an upward spraying geyser as men scattered in every direction.

Some of the men dove behind crates, while others hurled themselves to the ground and lay flat, with their arms over their heads. The sky thundered with a sound too loud to be understood, and in its wake came the ripping of fabric, the clatter of overturned gear, and the shouts of men who suddenly realized the front had arrived overhead.

At the command tent, Nieminen kicked open the flap and bellowed over the roar. "Rifles! Return fire! Bring down what you can!"

A corporal fired a flare skyward, red, and somewhere near the motor pool. A DShK opened up, the heavy machine gun rattling against its mount like a drum line made of thunder and hate, but it was too late to mount a defense. Captain Nieminen ground his teeth as he realized, *This wasn't a probe it was a strike.*

The Soviet bombers turned in low pairs, their bellies opening in sync. Fuel drums ignited and a stack of ammo crates cooked off in a stuttering chain of flashes. One of the mechanics, Jussi, the boy with the stammer, ran too slow. A bomb caught the earth five meters behind him. He didn't scream. He just vanished in a cloud of black earth and flame.

Above the Airfield – Minutes Later

The smoke was visible long before the runway. Veikko's gut twisted the moment he saw it, thick, oily columns rising in uneven stacks above the tree line. *Not drift smoke or fuel burn from a test engine. This was impact smoke. Hit-and-run fire.*

He angled the Fokker lower, the civilian still silent behind him. No one needed to explain anything now. As they cleared the final ridge, the field came into view, or at least what was left of it.

The southern end was cratered. One of the hangar tents had collapsed inward, blackened and torn. The command post had taken a glancing hit. Some of the tent's canvas was shredded, and a few of the poles were splintered.

Two Fokkers lay overturned near the dispersal line. Their frames were twisted like broken birds in the snow. One had landed upside down, the propeller sheared clean off and buried halfway into the ice. The other burned steadily, flames licking along the fuselage, its tail wedged into the splintered remains of a fuel sledge that had detonated on impact.

The heat shimmered in the freezing air, turning the rising smoke into a dark banner above the field. No one ran to extinguish it. There was nothing left to save.

Ground crew moved like ants below, their figures darting through smoke and fire with a desperation born of routine and terror. Some dragged the wounded across the snow, leaving ragged red trails behind them. Others clawed at the ground with shovels, boots, even bare hands as they tried to hack out crude fire lines in the ice to stop the flames from reaching the fuel stores.

A few had taken up rifles, standing exposed in the open, and firing blindly into the sky. They weren't aiming. They weren't expecting to hit anything. It was defiance, not strategy. A last gesture of resistance against the steel that thundered overhead. The bombers were already turning east, smoke trailing from one that must've caught flak on the way out. Veikko's hand tensed on the throttle. He could feel the tremor in the engine, not fear, or even rage. *Resolve.*

The landing strip was barely usable. Churned snow, debris, one corner torn into a shallow ditch by a missed drop. He came in hot. No clearance or pattern. Just instinct and control.

Hitting the snowpack, the wheels bounced once before catching. The Fokker skidded sideways, trailing a blade of churned snow as Veikko fought the rudder back into line. The officer behind him made a noise. It sounded like something between prayer and disbelief, but Veikko ignored it.

The moment the plane stopped moving, he killed the engine and was out of the cockpit before the propeller had fully stopped spinning. His boots hit snow, and the heat struck him like a wall. The fuel dump was still burning. He ran toward the line.

Pilot Tent – That Night

The fire had been contained, the wounded were carried off, and the dead were counted. Silence had returned. Inside the pilot tent, the warmth barely held. The stove hissed, overfed with damp wood that smoked more than it burned. A cracked lantern hung from the ridgepole, casting long shadows across the bunks.

Veikko sat near the back, his scarf still damp, boots streaked with mud and ash. He hadn't changed. He hadn't spoken since he walked in.

Rautio sat across from him, shoulders hunched, flight coat still buttoned tight. His eyes were locked on the stove. Kuusela leaned in the corner, his arms folded, and expression unreadable. Smoke curled from the corner of his mouth. The other corner held a smoldering cigarette. He didn't blink much. Not tonight.

Virtanen's bunk was empty. Someone had folded the blanket, but left his mug on the crate beside it, still half full, the rim streaked with a faint line of ash where the stove smoke had settled. Nobody touched it. Not because they hadn't noticed everyone had, but because in this place, reaching for a dead man's cup was bad luck. A kind of quiet curse. You didn't drink from it, didn't move it, didn't even glance at it too long. You left it where it was and prayed yours wouldn't be the next one left behind.

Veikko finally spoke. His voice was low and gravel dry. "They hit us because we changed."

Rautio looked up, eyes narrowing. "They wanted to see what the new pattern was," Veikko said. "So they provoked it. Drew us out. Me, you, all of us. Then they hit the soft spot."

Kuusela didn't argue. "They're not just adapting," Veikko said. "They're evolving."

He stared at the floorboards for a long moment, then leaned forward, elbows on his knees, hands dangling loose. "They won't wait for the next patrol. They'll come again, but not like this. Not bombers next time."

He looked up at the two men in front of him. "Next time, it'll be fighters."

The tent creaked, the sound low and tired. The noise sounded like old wood settling under weight it wasn't built to bear. Outside, the wind shifted, carrying with it the scent of snow and smoke, along with the faint, bitter sting of something that had gone wrong. The fire in the stove popped once, then went quiet again.

Somewhere east of the lines, beyond the reach of radios and reason, the Wolfpack circled through the mist, silent, patient, and learning. Every pass, every kill, every escape was another lesson. They weren't just hunting now. They were perfecting the craft of how to kill better.

Chapter 12

Forward Airfield, Outside Viipuri

December 5, 1939

The snow came overnight. It fell quiet and clean, blanketing the ruins in white like a nurse placing a sheet over a body. The cratered earth, burned tents, and the twisted bones of a fuel cart all lay buried beneath the illusion of calm. Nothing had been healed.

Veikko stood near the southern edge of the strip. His hands were shoved into his greatcoat pockets. Smoke still curled from the edge of the wreckage, lazy and gray against the falling flakes. Somewhere under that drift was the mess tent, or at least what was left of it.

Behind him, the camp was moving again. Tools clanged as crews cleared what they could. Orders were barked low and quick. Nobody shouted unless they had to.

The pilots had reassembled by the command post. No formal briefing. Just cold men waiting to be told where they might die next.

A truck engine rattled to a halt near the fuel drums. The cab door opened, and a fresh figure dropped down. The new pilot was young. *Too young*, thought Veikko

The young pilot carried a duffel that looked newer than his boots, and his face was clean, unlike everyone else at the base who hadn't showered in a week. He stood for a moment, looking around like he hadn't expected the front to look like this.

Sergeant Mika Honkala, the name had read on the dispatch. Transferred from a rear area squadron. Fourteen hours ago, he'd been warm, fed, and watching the war from the safety of someone else's mistakes. Now he was here.

He spotted Veikko and walked over. His posture was stiff, as his boots crunched the snow. He offered a salute that was sharp, but nervous. "Sergeant Honkala reporting, sir."

Veikko looked him over once. The boy was taller than he expected, but thinner, softer at the edges. No visible limp or burn marks and no broken stare. *Not yet.*

"Where'd they pull you from?" Veikko asked.

"Reserve Squadron 14, sir. Transport escort detail outside Lahti."

Veikko nodded once. "You'll be flying with Rautio."

Honkala hesitated. "Solo?"

"Loose pair. No formations. You stay in sight of each other. That's it."

Honkala glanced toward the flight line. "Is there a… briefing?"

"You're in it."

Flight Line – Thirty Minutes Later

The sun hadn't come up, but the sky had lightened just enough to reveal the wreckage in sharper detail. The soft gray light of early morning peeled back the illusion of calm the night's snowfall had offered. Burned canvas sagged under new drifts, half-melted fuel drums lay split open like broken eggs, and the dark streaks of smoke-stained snow marked where the fire had run unchecked. What had seemed, in darkness, like a chance to regroup now looked more like an aftermath. The damage was clearer in the half-light, more honest, and harder to ignore.

Rautio stood beside his Fokker, one hand resting on the wing strut, the other clenched into a fist inside his glove. His helmet hung around his neck. His face looked older than it had two days ago. Lined not with years, but with the consequences of war.

Veikko approached with Honkala trailing behind him, boots too loud on the packed snow. "Rautio," Veikko said, stopping just shy of the shadow cast by the wing. "You're flying Foxtrot Sector."

Rautio nodded. "Solo?"

"Loose pair. Honkala's your second."

Rautio's eyes shifted to the younger pilot.

Honkala straightened, saluted. "Sir."

Rautio's eyes narrowed. "You don't salute me fool. I'm a sergeant, same as you."

Honkala visibly wilted under the rebuke but remained silent. Veikko didn't bother with ceremony. "Same protocol. Stay loose, don't cross into Zulu grid. Watch for tree-line bait. No chatter unless you're bleeding."

Rautio didn't look away from Honkala. Not for a long beat. "Can he fly?" he asked quietly.

"He can land and shoot," Veikko said. "Whether he can do both when it matters—" he looked Honkala square in the eye "—is his problem."

Honkala swallowed hard but didn't flinch. Veikko leaned in closer, voice lower now, meant for Rautio alone. "If he breaks, you don't follow. You survive. Understood?"

Rautio nodded once. No bravado or questions. The flight cards were passed without ceremony. Rautio tucked his into the sleeve of his coat. Honkala glanced down at his hands, trembling just enough to be noticed. Rautio turned to his plane without another word. Honkala hesitated a half-second too long, then followed.

Above Sector Foxtrot – Late Morning

The clouds hung low over the forest like a warning. Thick, dark bands pressed against the treetops as if the sky itself were descending in slow, suffocating layers. They moved with a sluggish weight, heavy with ice and threat. The opaque mist blotted out the sun and bled the world of color.

Beneath them, the pine trees stood frozen and silent, their snow-caked branches drooping like arms burdened by unseen weight. The weak light was flat and directionless. It cast no shadows, only doubt. It was the kind of sky that held its breath before a kill. The kind of sky where things vanished.

Rautio flew point, keeping the lake chains on his left,

the foothills on his right. The Fokker's engine hummed at just under combat power, steady and even. Behind him, trailing wide and slightly high, came Honkala. Barely visible at times, but too visible at others.

Rautio keyed the mic once, then used two short bursts. *His spacing isn't right.*

The signal to correct formation spacing. Honkala adjusted late, then over-corrected. Rautio exhaled hard through his nose. *That young pup is going to get us killed before we sight the enemy.*

He shifted his trim and pushed lower, threading the line where mist met pine. The visibility was bad again today, white on white, soft shapes shifting where the forest pressed against the frozen rivers. *Perfect country for an ambush, or a grave.*

The patrol path wasn't formal anymore. No check-ins or rendezvous points. Just a sector, and the grim promise that if you saw something first, you might live to report it.

Rautio risked a glance back. Honkala was still there. Wings level. But he flew nervous and tight. *A dangerous combination.*

Honkala was a little too stiff in his turns. The kind of stiffness that breaks under pressure. "Loosen up," Rautio muttered under his breath. *This fool is not ready, and this isn't the time or place to fix that.*

Below, a stand of pine trees curved eastward. A narrow clearing followed. Beyond the clearing was a frozen bog choked with frost-slick reeds. In the middle of it, a long gouge scarred the ice. *Old crash site. Frozen over but not forgotten.*

Rautio didn't point it out as he said a silent prayer for

the pilot. He just banked left. Honkala followed, a second too slow.

It wasn't panic yet, but the thread was stretching. They continued northeast for another two minutes. Then—

Honkala's voice cracked through the radio. "Movement. Left side, eleven o'clock. Cloud band."

Rautio rolled slightly to get a look but saw nothing. Then the static hit. Sharp, sudden, jagged like a torn page across the headset, and then silence. No confirmation, repeat, contact or chance. Honkala was just gone.

Above Sector Foxtrot – Seconds Later

Rautio dropped altitude fast. He cut throttle, rolled shallow, and slipped into the lower cloud band where the air grew heavier and the trees blurred into gray knives below. Nothing on his left. No shapes or engines or flashes. Just the ever present cold.

He keyed the mic. "Honkala, say again."

No response. He pulled tighter into the turn, banking back toward Honkala's last heading. The wind howled over the canopy. His breath came fast now, fogging his goggles in short bursts. He wiped them clear with the back of his glove.

Still nothing. Then the mist parted and the world shifted. Ahead, just for a heartbeat, Rautio saw them. *Four fighters,*

The planes were high and spaced in a perfect staggered wedge. They weren't chasing Honkala. They were waiting above him, drifting slowly like vultures over a carcass not yet dead.

Then he saw Honkala's plane. Too low. Too tight in

the turn.
He was trying to climb, but wrong. Too steep and slow. *A panic move.*

One of the I-16s rolled out of the wedge. A clean dive. No hesitation. Rautio screamed into the mic. "Break, Honkala! Break right—"

The I-16 opened fire before Honkala moved. Tracer fire caught the Fokker in mid-climb. The tail snapped sideways. Then the left wing sheared. The plane rolled once, then dropped like a stone through the cloud layer.

No chute. Just a black streak vanishing into the forest. Rautio's heart kicked once, hard. Then another I-16 peeled off the top and began turning for him.

Rautio didn't think. He didn't climb or mourn. He slammed the throttle forward and yanked the stick into a brutal dive.

The Gs crushed his spine into the seat as the Fokker screamed through the cloud layer. The plane's wings shuddered against the sudden strain. Mist tore past in streaks as the altimeter spun. His teeth rattled in his skull.

Tracer fire stitched the air behind him. *Too close.*
He jinked left, then harder right, cutting low over the treetops. A pine branch ripped past his canopy. He could smell its resin even through the cold.

The I-16 stayed with him, one of them, maybe two. The others held back, climbing to reset. *They always reset. Clean flyers. Rehearsed killers.*

He couldn't out fly them in the open. He had to disappear. A frozen ravine split the terrain ahead, narrow and sharp like a wound in the forest. He dove for it without thinking.

Snow kicked up in white sheets as he skimmed the riverbed, weaving through tight turns and shadowed gullies. The wind became a scream in his ears. Behind him, an engine howled lower, but not as low.

They were above. Circling. Guessing.

He bled speed just enough to kill his profile, then dropped even lower until the trees loomed on either side like walls. Thirty seconds passed. Then sixty. No gunfire or chasing.

Just the hard knock of his heartbeat and the shallow rasp of his breath in the mask. He broke from the ravine, and climbed in a slow, shallow arc westward. His hands trembled on the stick, but they moved true.

The Wolfpack didn't follow. They'd already taken what they came for.

Forward Airfield – Early Afternoon

The sun was still hiding when Rautio landed. His approach was shallow, mechanical. The wheels kissed the hard pack, skidded once, and held. No bounce. Just contact. Snow sprayed behind him as the Fokker rolled to a stop at the northern end of the strip.

Mikkola didn't meet him. The line crew had already buried too many men this week. Rautio climbed down slowly, his limbs stiff. His scarf was half-untied. His mouth dry. He didn't speak.

He walked across the snow without turning his head, past the silent crewmen, past the fuel drums, and the crater where the latrine used to be. Inside the command tent, Nieminen was hunched over the field radio, pipe stem clenched between his teeth. The signal officer looked up first, then stepped aside.

Veikko was already there, arms folded, eyes hard. Rautio didn't salute. He just stood in the lamplight, his flight suit creaking as it thawed. "Honkala's gone," he said in a low and steady voice.

Nieminen nodded once, slowly. "What happened?" Veikko asked.

Rautio didn't pause. "They weren't chasing him. They were waiting. Stacked above. Perfectly placed. They let him see just enough to panic."

Nieminen blew a long stream of smoke through his nose. "A trap."

"A lesson," Rautio corrected. "For us."

He stepped forward, pointed to the grid sheet on the wall. "They picked the perfect spot. Bad visibility and shifting thermals. They had to know the terrain. It wasn't chance."

Nieminen stared at the map. "Then it wasn't a patrol."

Veikko said it first: "It was an execution."

Silence. The signal officer spoke next. "We picked up chatter. Soviet side. Scrambled half the words, but we caught a few, something about a 'Finn with a scar'... 'flies like a wolf but doesn't howl.' Might be nothing."

Veikko met Nieminen's eyes.

"It's not nothing," Nieminen said. "They're building profiles."

"Names," Veikko said. "Patterns. Personal targets."

"No," Rautio said quietly. "They're building doctrine. One kill at a time."

Chapter 13

Forward Airfield, Outside Viipuri

December 6, 1939

The mess tent still smelled faintly of scorched canvas. Half the benches were gone, cannibalized for firewood or barricades. The stove in the corner coughed out weak heat, barely enough to thaw fingers, but no one complained. No one talked much either.

Veikko sat at the corner table, hunched over a ledger of flight logs and mission debriefs. The paper was warped with moisture, ink blurred in places where snow or blood or both had soaked the margins. A cracked coffee mug steamed beside his elbow, untouched.

He wasn't reading anymore; he was reconstructing. *Three missions. Three patrols lost. Each in different sectors, on different days, but always the same kill pattern: Initial bait. Altitude misdirection. Second wave from above.*

He took a sip of coffee and continued his thought. *Each Finnish patrol had responded the same way. Predictably. By the book and the Soviets punished them for it.*

Veikko flipped a page, scanning a set of coordinates. *Then again. Same curve in the path. Same timing between contact and silence.*

He drew a line on the back of an old inventory form. Then another and finally a third.

They intersected. Not exactly, but close enough for doctrine. Across the tent, Nieminen entered, brushing snow from his shoulders, pipe clenched between his teeth. He paused when he saw Veikko's table, and the lines he was drawing.

"Not exactly poetry," Nieminen muttered.

"It's not art," Veikko said. "It's choreography."

He slid the logbook aside and held up the sketch. Three kill sites. Three vectors. Same slope, same pressure angle, same escape curve denied. "They're not improvising anymore," Veikko said. "They're performing."

Nieminen stepped closer, frowning. Veikko tapped the page. "Each time, the bait pulls the lead low. The strike comes from the rear-left high band. Always that quadrant. Then the collapse."

Nieminen took the sketch and studied it. "So, what, trap the trap?"

Veikko nodded. "We make ourselves look like prey. But this time, we're watching from above."

Nieminen's expression didn't change, but his shoulders eased slightly. "Can you do it without losing more men?"

"I think so," Veikko said. "But we'll need Kuusela, and I want Rautio."

Nieminen raised an eyebrow. "That boy's just barely holding together."

Veikko's voice was flat. "Then it's time he found out what he's made of."

Pilot Quarters – Nightfall

The wind rattled the canvas walls like something trying to claw its way inside. Inside the tent, the stove barely held a glow. The air stank of damp wool, cold metal, and old sweat. Boots steamed by the door. A single lantern flickered on a crate beside a mess tin half-filled with melted snow.

Kuusela sat with his elbows on his knees, sharpening a boot knife in slow, rhythmic pulls. Rautio leaned against the bunk post, arms crossed, helmet dangling from two fingers. His eyes hadn't quite come back from the day before.

Veikko stood between them, one glove tucked under his belt, the other holding a rolled map. "This isn't a patrol," he said. "It's a message."

He knelt, unrolled the map across the crate, and pinned the corners with a mug, a wrench, and a flare casing. He pointed to a thin, forest-choked sector west of Lake Ruokolahti. The terrain was jagged, the valleys deep.

"They expect us to probe and die. They're counting on us using the same formation and making the same mistake. This time, we let them think they've baited us."

Kuusela didn't look up from his knife. "What's the twist?"

"You," Veikko said. "You fly the line and make deliberate mistakes. Slight altitude inconsistencies. Late turns that sort of thing. The kind of sloppiness that looks like fatigue."

Kuusela finally looked up. "And if they believe it?"

"They'll pounce."

"And if they don't?"

"Then we fly another day."

Rautio shifted. "Where do I come in?"

"Here," Veikko said, tapping a bend in the ridge line. "North slope. You fly high cover, barely visible. If they jump him, you strike the tail. Disrupt their wedge and break the pattern."

"And you?" Kuusela asked.

"I'll be above the pattern. Watching the whole thing unfold."

Kuusela sheathed the knife with a soft *snick*. "You planning to shoot, or just narrate?"

"I'll shoot," Veikko said. "But only one target matters."

Rautio looked between them. "Chernyavin."

Veikko met his eyes. "He'll be there. He always watches first and I owe that bastard."

Kuusela slowly nodded once. "It's not about breaking the pack anymore. It's about cutting the head off."

Veikko folded the map again, pressing the creases flat. "We fly at dawn. No radios or second tries."

Rautio asked, "And if it goes wrong?"

Veikko's voice didn't waver. "Then we die loud."

Finally, the wind had stilled. The tent didn't creak. The stove barely breathed. Outside, the frost spread across the canvas like spiderwebs, silver veins catching the faint orange glow from the last piece of wood still burning.

Veikko sat alone at the end of his bunk, tightening the strap on his pistol belt. The buckle clicked softly. Beside him, the logbook lay open but untouched. There was nothing left to record that hadn't already been written in ash and wreckage.

Across the tent, Rautio checked the pressure in his gloves three times in a row. He wasn't trembling, not exactly. But his movements were too careful, like a man handling glass he didn't trust.

Kuusela leaned near the stove, his boots planted wide, shoulders forward. He held a piece of black bread between his fingers but hadn't bitten it. His eyes stayed fixed on the flames, distant and unmoving. No one spoke for a long time.

Finally, Rautio broke the silence. "We're really doing this."

Veikko didn't answer right away. Then: "We're already doing it."

Kuusela set the bread down on a crate, still untouched. "Three wolves circling a bigger one," he said. "Hope the bastard's hungry."

"He is," Veikko said, "but so are we."

Another silence settled in. Outside, boots crunched

past, quick and muffled. A little further away someone was dragging a fuel hose toward the edge of the hard pack. The kind of sound you heard every day. The kind of sound you might never hear again.

Rautio stood. "I'll check my plane."

Veikko didn't look up. "Do it slowly. Don't rush the ritual."

Rautio nodded and slipped out without a word. Kuusela followed a few seconds later, saying nothing. He took with him his coat, his knife, and his silence.

Veikko remained, hands resting on his knees, eyes fixed on the cooling stove. He whispered only once, to no one in particular: "This ends today."

The wind had returned but softer now. No shriek, no howl. Just a low exhale through the trees, cold enough to cut through scarf and leather. The sky was beginning to gray in the east, the color of unburned ash.

Three Fokkers sat lined up on the edge of the hard pack like sleeping hounds waiting for the leash to snap. Canvas covers were peeled halfway off, engines ticking as heat built under the cowling. Frost steamed from the exhaust ports in thin, ragged tendrils.

Veikko stood beside his machine, checking the flaps himself while Mikkola muttered about poor seals and thin oil. Rautio adjusted his trim tabs, silent, jaw locked tight. Kuusela smoked a half-cigarette with his gloves still on. His flight cap was already strapped on, and his goggles rested on his forehead. He looked like a man stepping into a duel, not a sortie.

"Clear to start!" someone called from the dispersal edge.

Veikko climbed into the cockpit. The leather of the Fokker's seat bit cold through his suit. He primed the fuel pump once, twice, three times. The engine coughed, caught, and growled to life.

Rautio's engine flared second. Then Kuusela's. Three planes. No chatter or ceremony. They taxied in line, wheels crunching through the crusted snow. Behind them, the airfield watched in silence, just breath clouds and hunched shoulders and the faint hiss of steam where frost met steel.

The runway stretched out white and uneven. No flares or ground crew signals. Just instinct and darkness.

Veikko opened the throttle. With an angry growl, the Fokker bucked forward. The wheels hammered over packed ice, then lifted. The machine took to the sky with a soft jolt. Rautio followed, then Kuusela.

They rose as three faint shadows into the fog, engines howling in staggered harmony, and disappeared into the mist without leaving a trace. The sky was the color of bone. Cloud bands lay in layered slabs above the frozen treetops, unmoving, thick enough to hide gods or killers.

Kuusela flew low and loose, his Fokker drifting between altitudes like a drunk on a frozen road. His heading was imprecise, his turns just a little wide, a little late. On paper: sloppy flying. In practice: bait.

He didn't speak or look back. His engine kept a steady pulse, but the attitude of the plane said tired, unguarded, vulnerable. Above and west, two kilometers distant and a hundred meters higher, Rautio flew wide arc cover. Watching. His eyes scanned constantly.

Higher still, Veikko flew at near idle, tucked above the upper mist layer, instruments darkened with soot and frost.

He didn't need them. He flew by shape and rhythm. Like a hunter waiting for breath to quicken in the underbrush.

Then it happened. A flicker behind the haze, east-northeast. A faint shadow that moved when it shouldn't. Then another with sharp wings and a short fuselage.

Veikko keyed the mic once. A single click. *They're here.*

He saw them fully now: four I-16s in a shallow V, dropping fast. Their angle was clean, and they accelerated quickly. The pattern was familiar. *Too familiar.*

Two peeled off to flank, curving left. One dipped lower, trying to draw Kuusela further down. The last hovered high, his engine throttled back, watching, just like before.

Chernyavin, Veikko thought.

Kuusela held steady. No panic or sudden acceleration. He let them close.

Veikko's grip tightened around the stick. *One more second—*

Then Kuusela broke. A snap roll into a shallow dive, tight and low. The Wolfpack surged after him.

"Now," Veikko said, voice sharp and clean in the headset.

Rautio dove first, slashing through the left-side flanker with guns blazing. Tracers tore across the I-16's canopy, glass and steel shattered. The Soviet rolled over, his plane smoking, and vanished downward.

Veikko pushed his throttle wide and fell from the cloud bank like a hammer. The sky ignited. The Fokker screamed as it plunged, its engine roaring. Frost sheared off the windscreen in chunks and disappeared into the gray murk. Veikko dropped straight through the cloud deck, mist shredding around him as the shape he'd been hunting locked into his sights.

Not a formation. Not a strike team. Just one plane now. One pilot. *Chernyavin.*

The Soviet ace flew high and aloof, just as before, his I-16 steady, riding the turbulence without correction. No weaving or reaction to Veikko's dive. He was playing the role of the commander, watching his wolves do the killing.

Only this time, the wolves were bleeding. Veikko leveled out, his air speed high, and the angle perfect. He rolled once to bleed speed, then corrected. Crosshairs found the center of the I16's fuselage. Chernyavin reacted late to Veikko's sudden appearance. A tilt, a throttle boost, but the trap had already closed. Veikko fired.

Tracers slashed forward as the Brownings chattered. The first burst caught nothing. The second chewed across the I-16's fuselage, just aft of the cockpit, then into the root of the right wing.

Smoke burst from the Soviet's engine cowling. A ragged trail. Chernyavin didn't panic. He didn't dive. He climbed. *Climbed!*

Veikko cursed and pulled up to follow, but the I-16 had already twisted, using the sun and vapor band to break line of sight. *These bastards always scattered when the pattern broke but Chernyavin? He escaped when it cracked. Always.*

"Rautio, status!" Veikko barked.

"Kuusela's clear. I got one off him. The other's running. I'm on your six."

"Break left and cover Kuusela."

"You going after him?"

"I have to."

Veikko rolled and dove again, following the smoke trail, but it was already thinning. Fading as it dissolved into sky. He pounded his fist on the coaming in frustration. *The ace was gone. Again.*

Forward Airfield – Late Morning, December 6, 1939

The wind had picked up again. It swept snow across the runway in low, hissing veils. The sky was still gray, the light still flat, but something in the air had changed.

Veikko's Fokker came in fast and low. The wheels struck the strip and bounced once, hard, before catching. The tail wobbled but he held it, rudder steady. Rautio landed next, a clean touchdown. Behind him, Kuusela rolled in slower, engine coughing smoke.

Veikko taxied his plane to the northern dispersal line where Mikkola stood waiting. The crew chief's jaw was clenched, and his rough calloused hands were jammed deep into his coat.

Mikkola met Veikko at the wing with his usual scowl already in place. "You didn't exactly baby her," he muttered, eyes scanning the gouges along the cowling.

Veikko unstrapped his flight helmet and dropped it on the wing. "She held."

"For now." Mikkola ran a gloved hand along the puckered edge where a round had clipped the engine housing. His fingers twitched, just slightly. "This one's going to keep me up tonight."

"You still wrapping that burn?" Veikko asked, nodding toward the man's bandaged forearm.

Mikkola grunted. "Only when the scabs crack open in the cold. So every day."

Veikko gave a dry half-smile. "At least you've got something to complain about."

"Not if you keep flying like this," Mikkola said, straightening. "I won't have any plane left to complain about."

One by one, the three pilots climbed down. The crew moved in fuel lines, engine checks, quick glances exchanged under breath clouds. The ritual of survival. The gods of maintenance appeased by silence and motion.

Veikko pulled off his gloves slowly. The veteran pilot looked skyward, but his mind was still back in the fight. He could still see Chernyavin's fighter spiraling through smoke, damaged but flying. *Not a ghost anymore.* He smiled at the thought.

He turned as Captain Nieminen approached, coat flapping against the wind.

"Well?" Nieminen asked.

Veikko didn't answer immediately. He reached into the cockpit, pulled a twisted fragment of metal from the footwell, and held it out. The edge was scorched.

Nieminen took it. Examined it. Then looked up.

"His?" he asked.

Veikko nodded once. "I hit him."

Nieminen exhaled. Long and slow. For the first time in

two weeks, the silence at the airfield didn't feel like dread. It felt like hope.

Chapter 14

Dawn

Forward Command Tent, Dawn

December 7, 1939

The cold came early that morning. Not the sharp kind that bit skin, but the deep cold that pressed into the joints and settled behind the ribs. The kind that made you feel like the air itself had stopped moving.

Inside the command tent, the kerosene lamp guttered against the draft seeping in around the seams. Its glow flickered across the field table, casting a dull shine on the oil-slicked map beneath. Red Xs marked where planes had died. Grease-pencil arrows marked where others had barely returned.

Veikko stood at the table's edge, gloves tucked into his belt, and his cap pulled low over his brow. He held a small canvas pouch in one hand. He set it down without ceremony, then opened it.

Inside lay three items: A scorched piece of engine

cowling. A twisted length of aluminum with red paint still clinging to one edge, and a bolt, sheared by heat and force, blackened to near coal.

"Chernyavin's fighter," Veikko said.

Silence. Captain Nieminen stepped forward. His pipe stem was clenched in the side of his mouth. He didn't touch the parts. Just studied them. Then he met Veikko's eyes.

"Proof?"

"He bled," Veikko said. "Enough to stagger him. Not enough to stop him."

Around the tent, the squad leaders watched without speaking. No questions or optimism. Just the tension of men measuring risk by the day and running out of coin.

Nieminen leaned over the table and tapped a point east of Ruokolahti. "They're healing. You think it'll take him long to rebuild?"

"No," Veikko said. "He'll fly again soon, and when he does, he'll bring more like him. New pilots trained under his doctrine. If we wait, they'll become stronger. Next time, we won't be able to break the pattern."

"What do you propose?"

Veikko didn't hesitate. "We flip it."

He picked up the sheared bolt and pointed it like a knife toward the northern edge of the map. "We go into their grid. Their airspace. Their kill zones, but we stop patrolling. No sweeps or grid coverage."

"Then what?"

"Ambushes. Targeted strikes. We don't look for patterns. We create them. Confuse and harass. Disrupt command flow, and we don't fly like wolves anymore. We fly like ghosts."

Someone at the back scoffed. "That's suicide."

Veikko turned. "So is waiting. Except that version's slower."

Nieminen stepped back. He studied the parts again. Then the men.

"Select your wing," he said. "Tight pairs only. No chatter unless it's to confirm a kill or call for fire. Burn their doctrine to the ground."

Veikko nodded. They weren't being hunted anymore. They were sharpening their teeth.

Above Grid Echo – Noon, December 7, 1939

The sky was thin and colorless over Grid Echo, a lifeless sheet of white pressing down on the frost-bitten treetops. Two Fokker D.XXIs moved like blots of ink in the void, staggered, uneven, and very alone.

They weren't patrolling. They were playing the role of bait. Sergeant Otso Niemi flew high cover, his breath frosting the inside edge of his scarf, eyes locked on the wisping cloud bands below. His wingman, Sergeant Lauri Saarinen, flew ragged and low dipping erratically, banking with the kind of fatigue that begged for attention.

"Cut throttle a touch more," Niemi said over the mic, voice low and clipped. "You're still flying like you're trying to get home."

"I am trying to get home," Saarinen muttered.

"Then act like you won't."

They passed over a frozen river bend, a funnel of terrain where more than one patrol had vanished. Saarinen began a shallow, wobbling turn, loose on the rudder. Below him, the treetops shifted and above, Niemi caught it.

"High, three o'clock. Four, maybe five. Staggered climb."

"I see them," Saarinen said. His voice cracked.

Niemi peeled off hard, banking and climbing in a wide arc to flank the formation. Tracers lanced the air behind Saarinen, the bait had worked. So had the trap.

"Don't climb yet," Niemi snapped. "Stay level. Bleed them in."

"I can't—"

"You can. Hold steady. I've got the top gun."

Saarinen dropped another ten meters. The Soviet fighters followed but not recklessly. They knew the rhythm. Press the prey low. Let the high ship kill him clean.

Niemi cut inside the arc.

He pulled tight, the Gs thudding into his chest, and brought the Fokker's nose up into the belly of the high I-16. His guns flared.

The rounds found steel and skin. The Polikarpov burst into smoke, its right wing twisting free in mid-roll. It tumbled from the sky like a kicked hornet, black smoke unfurling behind it.

"One!" Niemi barked into the mic, but the others were already moving.

Saarinen tried to roll but it was too late. A burst caught his tail. The Fokker kicked sideways, the engine choking, and slammed into the treetops with a sickening crunch that Niemi felt through his own ribs.

"Lauri!"

There was no answer. Just mist, branches, and flame curling from the forest below.

Above Grid Kilo – Midafternoon, December 7, 1939

The wind carried teeth this high up. Rautio flew alone, just beneath the haze band, where the air shimmered in glassy layers and the light lay flat as a blade. No wingman or instructions. Just a patch of sky and his own instinct.

The Fokker's engine hummed steadily. His hands rested loose on the stick, light and ready. He'd stopped gripping it too hard. It was almost as if he were trying to out-muscle the sky. Let it move first, he'd learned.

Below, the frozen lakes glittered. A long stretch of tree line pressed westward, curving into a crescent like a sickle. He followed it, cutting arcs that looked lazy but were deliberate. He followed Veikko's advice for this flight, controlled sloppiness.

The wolf pack didn't pounce right away. That was the new trick. They let you think you were alone. Let you breathe and lured you deeper into their den.

Then they bit. Rautio dipped his right wing, let it hang slightly too long. The kind of mistake that screamed fatigue. A good pilot would correct. A perfect predator would dive, and one did.

The shadow came from the left. Sharp and quick. An I-16 in a steep dive. No flare, or hesitation, just a clean strike angle.

Rautio didn't panic. He banked hard, a bit early. Too early for a real rookie. He turned into the attack, cutting below the Soviet's firing arc. The tracers whipped wide.

He rolled left, half-inverted, kicked the rudder, and came up behind the dive angle just as the Soviet pilot leveled. They matched speed for a second. Rautio fired.

The Brownings chattered. Tracers chewed across the I-16's right flank, punching into the cowling. The Soviet jerked hard, but it was too late. Smoke spilled from the engine bay, then flame.

The fighter banked, bleeding altitude fast. Rautio didn't follow. He climbed, fast and sharp, scanning the mist. He saw nothing.

He keyed the mic. "Contact neutralized. Solo target. No support spotted."

The silence that followed was the clearest affirmation he could ask for.

He pulled higher into the cloud bank, heart thudding steady. *That had been clean. Not lucky. Clean.* He smiled as he thought, *I'm not bait anymore.*

Forward Airfield – Dusk, December 7, 1939

The sun hadn't set, but the light was already gone. A pale smear over the trees marked the edge of the day, fading behind the cloud line like breath on glass. The snow reflected none of it, just a dull, gray sheen stretched across the frozen field like the skin of something long dead. Shadows pooled early in the corners of tents and beneath the wings of grounded aircraft, while the wind pushed through the trees in slow, whispering waves.

Veikko stood near the northern end of the runway, one boot on a snow-covered crate, scarf pulled high. His eyes tracked the distant tree line, where mist clung low, and the wind carried a brittle hum. The others were back, Kuusela, and Rautio. Neither of them was speaking.

They'd made contact and killed. The silence that followed didn't feel like triumph.
It felt like a question.

Rautio broke it first. His voice low, almost as if speaking might conjure what they'd just escaped. "One of them came at me. I turned into him and then got on his tail." He smiled. "The Russian bastard didn't live very long after that."

"Discipline's slipping," Kuusela muttered, adjusting his gloves, "Or they're tired. Either way, they're not pressing like they used to."

No one commented. Veikko's eyes never left the trees. "They're bleeding, but it doesn't feel like a win."

"It's not," Kuusela said. "It's a pause. They'll come back sharper."

Rautio glanced over. "How many more of them are there?"

Veikko answered without looking. "Enough. Most Soviet pilots aren't worth a damn, but anyone trained by Chernyavin is highly skilled. Fortunately for us, the number of those pilots will be limited. "

They stood a while longer in the hush, the distant tree line silent and still, as if waiting. Then, something faint through the mist. A new sound began to rise. A hum at first, distant and uncertain, like the beginning of a storm that hadn't yet decided where to fall.

Veikko straightened. "They're not finished."

No one argued. Then, they heard it too. Not the thunder of bombers. Not the chop of an I-16 diving. Something coming in fast and low.

Veikko turned. Nieminen was already striding out from the command tent, pipe clenched between his teeth. "Eyes up," Nieminen growled.

A shadow passed low over the trees. Small and sleek. The plane was too fast for a bomber and too clean for a scout. Just a blur that barely cleared the smokestacks jutting from the tops of the tents. The plane banked hard and disappeared before the crews could aim a rifle.

No bombs, gunfire or message dropped.

Just a deliberate and measured fly-by. Veikko stepped into the open, watching the sky where it vanished. The shape had been familiar. The hum of the engine was not one of theirs.

"Was that a recon pass?" someone muttered.

"No," Veikko said quietly. "That was a lesson."

Nieminen joined him. "What did it teach?"

Veikko didn't look away. "That they're still watching. Still learning and despite their losses today they're not done."

The wind shifted again. The smell of fuel and fire drifted across the field and somewhere out there, cloaked

in fog and doctrine, the Wolfpack circled again alive,
evolving, and still sharpening its teeth.

Chapter 15

Forward Airfield, Outside Viipuri

December 8, 1939

The wind howled across the field like something wounded. Snow swept sideways in long, low sheets, scouring the tents and scarring the ridge lines with fresh drift. The air smelled of oil, scorched canvas, and expectation.

Inside the command tent, the map lay pinned beneath a wrench and a mug of tea gone cold. Veikko leaned over it, gloved fingers tapping a narrow valley east of Ruokolahti. The paper was creased and soft from use, stained with old coffee and the imprint of a hundred decisions made under duress.

"This is where we finish it," he said, voice low.

Kuusela stood opposite him, arms crossed, the collar of his flight coat pulled high against the chill. His eyes tracked the curve of the river bend on the page. "They'll bite?"

"They always do," Veikko replied. "If the bait bleeds

just right."

Rautio stood slightly back, not leaning on anything. He wasn't fidgeting or smiling. He hadn't smiled in days, but his eyes were clearer than they'd been since Halme went down. Focused now. Not fearless, but willing.

"What's my role?" he asked.

"Knife through the spine," Veikko said.

He turned the map toward them both, dragging a gloved finger along a narrow line just north of the bait sector. "Kuusela flies the line. Tight but not perfect. A little wobble. A late climb here." He tapped twice. "Just enough to look tired."

Kuusela nodded once. "I've had practice."

"You'll get one pass," Veikko said. "Maybe two. If they think you're alone, they'll wait to collapse. When they do, Rautio hits the tail wedge, and I isolate Chernyavin."

"And if it's not Chernyavin?" Rautio asked.

"Then we make it Chernyavin's funeral anyway," Kuusela said.

No one laughed. Veikko straightened. "No radios unless you're dying. No second flights or falling back. This is the trap."

Outside, the snow deepened. Somewhere in the sky above them, the Wolfpack circled. Still waiting and learning, but so were they.

Over Sector Echo, 1130 Hours – December 8, 1939

The sky had the texture of steel wool gray, coarse, and scouring from the inside out. Kuusela flew alone. His

Fokker rattled a little more than it should've. That was intentional. The rudder trim was left slightly off. His altitude wandered by a few meters every pass. Intentional. He dipped a second too late into each turn and made a few course corrections visible enough to catch the eye of a watcher with a practiced eye. Also, intentional.

The entire patrol was a lie. One designed to smell like fatigue, taste like sloppiness, and bleed just enough credibility to draw the kill. He passed over a frozen marsh near Grid 3-Charlie, letting the nose drift slightly low before correcting. Nothing too clean or sharp. A predator would be watching for the correction.

Behind him and above, Rautio was somewhere to the northeast, flying quiet. He was invisible. Veikko would be even higher. Ghostlike.

Kuusela adjusted his trim again and let the Fokker drift left a few degrees. The kind of course deviation that says he's tired, sloppy, and alone. He wasn't.

The world below blurred past: snow-crusted pines, ice-locked lakes, the skeletal outlines of broken trees scorched from recent artillery barrages. This sector hadn't seen the ground war, not really, but it had seen the sky burn.

Kuusela exhaled slowly, then dipped the wing. He was entering the box now. If the Soviets were watching, and he knew they were, they'd see the gap. The pattern and most importantly the mistake.

He was giving them the window. Now all that was left was to wait, and bleed enough just to make them come down for the kill.

Sector Echo – December 8, 1939 – 1150 Hours

The first flicker came at Kuusela's seven o'clock, high,

sharp, and deliberate.

A glint of light that didn't belong to the clouds or the sun. He didn't turn or flinch. Just let the Fokker drift a little wider on the next leg, as if he'd missed his mark.

Then came the second shape directly above him now. Holding steady. They were pacing him. He couldn't see the others yet, but he didn't need to. They were setting up. *They'd taken the bait.*

His hands tightened on the stick, not in fear, but focus. He was playing the part of the tired patrolman. The drifting solo. If he did it right, they'd collapse in a classic wedge, two low, one high, maybe a fourth hovering as shepherd.

The same structure. The same deadly clockwork. Except this time, the mouse had teeth.

Kuusela keyed the mic once—*click*. Then a second time—*click*. That was it.

High above, Rautio's headset hissed with the double burst. His fingers twitched inside his gloves, his thumb resting on the trigger switch. He saw them now.

Four I-16s. Pattern perfect. Tight wedge forming to Kuusela's east. The lead was higher, just under the cloud line, circling to watch. *Always watching. Chernyavin.*

Veikko saw him too. From even higher still, his Fokker ghosted above the top band of cloud, trim neutral, throttle barely cracked. His breath fogged inside the mask. His crosshairs already moving to lead the enemy.

Rautio rolled right and slipped into position behind the lower pair. He wouldn't strike yet. Not until the high cover committed.

Below, Kuusela dipped slightly, let the wing shudder, and pulled late into the next turn. It was enough. The upper fighter moved. A sharp break as the enemy plane rolled into a dive.

They thought they had him, but they were wrong. Rautio's hand snapped the throttle open. His Fokker surged forward. *Time to break the pack.*

Sector Echo – 1152 Hours – Over the Frozen Forests

The I-16 dove hard, clean, fast, and practiced. Kuusela saw the glint of its gun first, then the shape. The Soviet fighter snapped down from the clouds like a spear thrown from God's hand, muzzle already flashing.

Tracer rounds screamed past Kuusela's left wing. He didn't roll. It wasn't time. He wanted the lead to get cocky first.

The second I-16 followed the dive, lower, tighter. The trap had closed and they hadn't noticed the jaws. Above and behind, Rautio kicked into a steep descent, throttle wide, angle perfect. The Wolfpack's rear was exposed for half a heartbeat and that's all he needed.

He lined up the trailing I-16, the one hanging back to shepherd the kill, and fired. The Brownings chattered. Tracers ripped through the sky, clean and straight.

The Soviet plane twitched, then shuddered. Smoke burst from its engine cowling, black and oily. The fighter peeled off, arcing downward in a spin, vanishing behind the tree line without flame or flare. *One down.*

The others flinched. The formation cracked, not fully, not yet, but enough. The lead pilot hesitated. That was his mistake. Veikko dropped through the cloud layer like thunder.

He came in silent, fast, and straight. The high I-16, Chernyavin's bird, was already rolling left, breaking to regain height and cover. Veikko matched the move.

The cold bit into his knuckles as he adjusted trim and throttle simultaneously. He could feel the strain in the airframe, the tension in the stick. It was like wrestling the sky itself for control.

Below, Kuusela rolled out of the dive and juked sideways, fast and clean. He wasn't the prey anymore. He was the bait that bit back.

Rautio kept climbing. He was behind another one now but let him go. He was playing shadow to Kuusela. The others would turn, but not in time.

Above them all, Veikko drew his bead on the commander's I-16. It wasn't a perfect shot. It didn't have to be. He squeezed the trigger, a short and tight burst.

The tracers walked up toward the I-16's tail, chewing through fabric and steel. The Soviet pulled hard left, too hard, and stalled for a second. Just a second. It was enough.

Veikko pulled up, rolled inverted, and came over the top. The kill wasn't clean, but the command was broken. Below, the Wolfpack scattered before them. He smiled. *Their boots are filled with piss.*

The trap had worked, but the duel wasn't over.

Over Sector Echo – 1154 Hours

Veikko rolled hard to port, chasing the tail of the high fighter as it spiraled out of formation. He didn't need to confirm the markings or the flight pattern. He knew who it was. The calm, deliberate evasive turn. The refusal to break under pressure. The unwillingness to commit until the kill was certain. *Chernyavin.*

Two years melted away in an instant. The frozen forests of Karelia transformed into the sunbaked plains of Spain. For a heartbeat, Veikko was back in that Fiat CR.32, desperately trying to match a master who was three moves ahead. His left shoulder throbbed with remembered pain. The same shoulder that had shattered when he'd slammed into Spanish soil. The same Soviet pilot circled above him now, his I-16 slipping through the air with elegant precision.

Not this time, Veikko thought.

He wasn't the green pilot who'd been effortlessly outmaneuvered over Valencia anymore. He'd spent two years preparing for this moment, studying the wreckage of his defeat, analyzing every move Chernyavin had made. In his mind, he'd flown this dogfight a thousand times.

The Soviet ace didn't climb. He slid sideways into a tight, flat corkscrew that bled speed without giving altitude. A veteran's move. He was drawing Veikko down, testing his patience, trying to bait an overrun exactly as he had in Spain.

"I know your dance now," Veikko whispered behind his oxygen mask. "I've been watching."

He mirrored the maneuver, holding speed, riding high. They circled each other in the gray, two wolves on opposite banks of a frozen river. This time, Veikko wasn't prey. This time, he was the hunter.

Then Chernyavin snapped into a climb. Veikko followed. His engine screamed and the airframe shuddered under the strain. Frost shook loose from the canopy frame.

The two aircraft clawed for altitude in lockstep, their wings nearly mirrored as they rose into the glare above the mist. Ice shimmered on Veikko's struts. Wind tore at them like teeth. Higher and higher they rose until the climb broke into a hammerhead.

Chernyavin stalled first. He flipped downward, rolling into a dive, and Veikko went with him, nose to tail. They cut through the mist in a vertical chase. The world shrank to a tunnel of air and speed. The G-forces crushed their chests. Their blood throbbed behind their eyes.

Chernyavin pulled up hard. Veikko stayed on him. He didn't shoot. Not yet. Not until it was clean.

They arced again, looping wide over a frozen lake below. Tracers flashed, Cheryavin was too early. A burst of frustration. A flicker of doubt. *He's tiring.*

Veikko rolled inside and flattened his turn. The Soviet's I-16 was slower now, sloppy on the pitch. Then came the window. The I-16 over-banked on a shallow climb.

Veikko pressed the trigger. His Brownings barked once, short, and violent.

The rounds punched through the Soviet's right-wing root and into the engine cowling. The I-16 lurched, rolled over, and trailed smoke. Veikko climbed past it, banked, and circled. He waited, but this time, there was no recovery dive. No ghost slipping into mist.

Chernyavin's fighter spiraled once then twice before it caught a treetop with its wingtip. The spin collapsed. The forest below erupted in a brief, sharp bloom of fire and smoke.

Veikko circled once. Then pulled west. The sky felt emptier than it had in weeks.

Forward Airfield – Early Afternoon – December 8, 1939

The sun had crawled low behind a gauze of clouds by the time Veikko set the Fokker down.
The wheels hit hard, once, then again, and bit into the frozen strip. He let the tail settle, taxied without rush, without radio calls. There was no need. They'd seen the smoke rise in the east.

Mikkola stood at the dispersal line, wrench in hand, scarf pulled high around his scarred neck. He didn't wave. Just tracked the Fokker with his eyes as it rolled to a stop.

Veikko climbed down slowly. His gloves were stiff with sweat and frost. The wind caught the scarf at his throat and flung it sideways like a signal flag.

Mikkola stood at the dispersal line, a wrench in one hand, scarf pulled high over the burn scars that streaked the left side of his neck. He didn't wave or step forward. He just tracked the Fokker's approach with his hard and unreadable eyes.

The engine sputtered, coughed, and died. Veikko climbed down slowly, boots thudding into the packed snow. His gloves were stiff with sweat and frost. The wind caught the scarf at his throat and yanked it sideways like a signal flag.

Mikkola didn't wait. "Was it him?"

Veikko didn't answer right away. He peeled off one glove, flexed his fingers, and looked past Mikkola toward the cratered field. "It was."

Mikkola's jaw twitched. He stepped forward half a pace, his wrench forgotten at his side. "And?"

Veikko met his eyes. "He's not flying home."

Mikkola exhaled once through his nose. No grin or fist pump. Just a slow nod, the kind that came from burying too many men to celebrate lightly. "Good," Mikkola said. Then, quieter: "Damn good."

He looked up at the sky, gray and featureless, then back at Veikko. "Took long enough."

Veikko gave the faintest shrug. "He was a hard kill."

Mikkola looked down at the Fokker, noting a fresh scar scored across the leading edge. "I see you gave me more work to do."

He turned, started walking toward the hangar without another word. Halfway there, he stopped, glanced back over his shoulder. "Glad you made it back," he said. "Would've been a bitch digging another grave in the frozen ground."

Veikko didn't smile, but his voice carried as he set off toward the other two pilots waiting at the edge of the flight line. "I bet."

Kuusela was already there, leaning against a drum crate, arms crossed, eyes shaded by his cap. He didn't speak, but when their eyes met, he gave a single, small nod. Rautio stood a few paces back, face unreadable. He looked at Veikko the way soldiers look at survivors: half respect, and half warning.

Veikko didn't speak until he reached the edge of the flight line. Then, softly, he said, "It's done."

No cheers, laughter or backslaps. Just the wind picking up again, stirring the snow into thin spirals that danced between the wheels of the parked aircraft. Chernyavin was dead, but no one said his name.

Not because they feared it, but because they knew, deep down, someone else would wear it soon enough. The war was far from over, but for the moment, the skies over Viipuri were quiet.

Northern Claws: Combat Tales from Finland's Skies

Episode 1

First Blood

Lieutenant Eino Luukkanen's boots crunched through the predawn frost as he made his way toward the Fokker D.XXI fighter, its silhouette a dark smudge against the gunmetal sky. The bitter cold of November 30th, 1939, seeped through his flying jacket. Snow had fallen overnight, dusting the wings of the aircraft with a fine powder that the ground crew was busily sweeping away.

The blue and white roundel emblem of the Finnish Air Force stood in stark contrast to the olive drab fuselage. Luukkanen ran a gloved hand along the leading edge of the wing, feeling the cold aluminum beneath his fingertips. For three months, they'd been at heightened readiness, practicing, preparing, waiting. But this morning felt different somehow.

Mechanics worked with quiet efficiency, their breath forming clouds in the frigid air. The thermometer had shown minus fifteen Celsius when Luukkanen had checked it in the operations building. Typical Finnish winter. He stamped his feet to keep the blood flowing and nodded to his mechanic, Sergeant Urpo Raunio.

"How is she this morning?" Luukkanen asked, patting the fuselage of his fighter, designated FR-104.

"Oil's thick as molasses, Lieutenant, but she'll fly." Raunio's face was ruddy from the cold. "Guns are cleaned and loaded. Full ammunition."

"Good." Luukkanen nodded, studying the aircraft. The Fokker D.XXI wasn't the newest fighter in the world, with its fixed landing gear and fabric-covered fuselage, but its four 7.62mm machine guns gave it reasonable firepower, and it was maneuverable enough to hold its own, provided the pilot knew what he was doing.

"I'll be back shortly," he said, turning toward the "alert tent," a canvas structure near the edge of the Immola airfield that served as their ready room.

Inside, a dozen pilots huddled around the iron stove in the center, nursing steaming cups of coffee. The tent flap closed behind him, shutting out the biting wind.

"Morning, Eino." Tatu Huhanantti, his deputy flight commander, handed him a chipped enamel mug filled with coffee that was black as tar. "Sleep well?"

"Like the dead," Luukkanen replied, gratefully accepting the scalding brew. He took a careful sip, feeling it burn all the way down. "Any news?"

Tatu's face was drawn, his eyes ringed with shadows. He lowered his voice. "Just rumors. Something about bombs falling on Helsinki."

Luukkanen stiffened. "Confirmed?"

"Not officially." Tatu glanced toward Captain Magnusson, who was deep in conversation with a signals officer in the corner of the tent. "But the radio traffic has tripled in the last hour."

Lieutenant Vic Pyötsiä looked up from the map he was

studying. "If it's true, we're at war."

The words hung in the air between them. War. The thing they'd been preparing for, dreading, and in some dark corner of their souls, anticipating. The ultimate test of all their training.

"War changes a man," said Captain Magnusson, who had finished his conversation and overheard Vic's comment. "You're not really a fighter pilot until you've faced the enemy and lived to tell about it."

Luukkanen contemplated this as he warmed his hands on the mug. He had over a thousand hours of flight time, but not a single one in combat. How would he react when the moment came? Would his hands shake too much to aim if he froze when another human being was in his gunsight?

"Weather report," announced Sergeant Major Rissanen, entering with a clipboard. "Ceiling at two thousand feet. Temperature holding steady. Wind northwest at ten knots."

Magnusson nodded. "Standard alert patrol schedule today. Luukkanen, your flight is up first. Readiness in thirty minutes."

"Yes, sir."

Luukkanen drained his coffee and set the mug down. He'd done this routine dozens of times since they'd moved to Immola in October. Listening and waiting, ready to scramble if Russian aircraft crossed the border. So far, it had only been reconnaissance flights, that probed and tested Finnish airspace. If the rumors about Helsinki were true, everything had changed.

"Come on," he said to his flight members. "Let's check

the birds."

Outside, the sky had lightened fractionally, turning from black to deep blue. The stars were fading one by one. Dawn wouldn't fully break for another hour at this latitude and time of year. Luukkanen and his three pilots walked in silence to their aircraft. Each man was lost in his own thoughts.

The preflight inspection was thorough, but quick. A ritual Luukkanen had performed hundreds of times. Luukkanen checked the control surfaces, inspected the four 7.62 mm machine guns, and verified that the ammunition feeds lacked safety pins. The Mercury radial engine's cowling was cold to the touch.

"She's ready, sir," said Raunio, standing at attention beside the Fokker. "Full fuel. Ammunition checked and loaded."

"Thank you, Sergeant." Luukkanen nodded, trusting the mechanic's expertise. Raunio had been with him since his days flying Bristol Bulldogs. The man could diagnose an engine problem just by listening to it.

The pilots returned to the alert tent to wait. Luukkanen reviewed his maps, tracing the patrol route they would fly if ordered up, a standard circuit over the Karelian Isthmus, watching for any incursion from the east. The minutes ticked by with agonizing slowness. He checked his watch: 09:15.

Suddenly, the door to the operations building flung open. Colonel Riku Lorentz, the regimental commander, strode across the field toward them. Even at a distance, Luukkanen could see the tension in the colonel's bearing. Something had happened.

Lorentz burst into the alert tent, not bothering to

remove his cap or gloves. His face was flushed, his eyes bright. Without preamble, he drew his service revolver and fired a single shot into the ceiling of the tent.

The report was deafening in the enclosed space. Coffee mugs clattered to the floor as men jumped to their feet.

"This morning at 06:15 hours, Russian forces crossed our country's borders!" Lorentz announced, his voice cutting through the stunned silence. "Soviet bombers hit Helsinki several hours ago and at this moment a number of enemy aircraft are reported to be heading in the direction of Viipuri!"

Luukkanen felt his heart rate double instantly. This was it. The moment they had been preparing for.

Captain Magnusson stepped forward. "Lieutenant Luukkanen, get your flight in the air immediately. Intercept over Viipuri."

Luukkanen was already moving, as adrenaline surged through his veins. "Yes, sir!"

He burst from the tent, his pilots close behind, sprinting toward their aircraft. The mechanics had heard the commotion and were already preparing for immediate takeoff. Luukkanen's mind raced with calculations, distance to Viipuri, fuel consumption, altitude for interception, automatic thoughts drilled into him through years of training.

He reached his Fokker and climbed onto the wing, swinging himself into the cockpit with practiced ease. Raunio was already cranking the inertia starter, the heavy flywheel spinning up with a high-pitched whine. When it reached speed, he engaged it with the engine. The Mercury coughed once, twice, then roared to life with a cloud of blue smoke. The entire airframe vibrated with its power.

Raunio disconnected the external starter and gave him a thumbs-up. Luukkanen returned the gesture, then slipped on his flying helmet and goggles. The familiar smell of leather, oil, and canvas enclosed him.

For a moment, a stab of doubt pierced his concentration. What if his guns jammed or he couldn't find the enemy? Would he freeze at the critical moment?

The thoughts vanished as quickly as they came. There was no time for doubt now. He was the flight leader. Three other men were following him into combat. Finland was under attack.

He released the brakes and taxied to the takeoff position, the other three Fokkers falling into line behind him. The control tower flashed a green light. Luukkanen pushed the throttle forward, feeling the surge of acceleration as the fighter began to move.

The Fokker D.XXI gathered speed, bumping over the frozen ground. At eighty miles per hour, Luukkanen eased back on the stick, and the aircraft lifted smoothly into the air. The ground fell away beneath him. He was airborne and committed to battle.

The other fighters joined him, forming up over Immola Lake. Luukkanen banked toward Viipuri, setting course at 186 miles per hour. He leveled off just beneath the cloud base at two thousand feet. The formation was tight, and professional. He felt a surge of pride in his flight.

There was no going back now. Whatever waited for them at Viipuri, they would face it together. The radio crackled with static. "Immola to Luukkanen. Russian bombers reported over the Viipuri rail yard. Multiple aircraft."

"Acknowledged," Luukkanen replied, then switched to

the flight frequency. "Keep your eyes open. We're heading into a fight."

As they flew, Luukkanen's thoughts turned to his Fokker. It was sturdy, reliable, and maneuverable. The four machine guns gave it respectable firepower. In the right hands, it could hold its own, but would his hands be the right ones?

He pushed the doubt aside, focusing instead on the aircraft's familiar responses. The way the stick vibrated slightly at this speed and the sweet spot in the throttle setting where the engine ran smoothest. The faint smell of gun oil from the weapons in the cowling was almost relaxing. This machine was his partner, his shield, his weapon. They had trained together for hundreds of hours. Now they would fight together.

Viipuri appeared ahead, a sprawl of buildings beside the Gulf of Finland. Even from miles away, Luukkanen could see plumes of black smoke rising from the city center. His jaw tightened. Those were Finnish homes burning.

"Here we go," he muttered, more to himself than to his silent radio.

At 09:45, they reached the outskirts of Viipuri. Luukkanen scanned the sky frantically, searching for the enemy bombers. Nothing. Just the sullen clouds above and the burning city below.

"Spread out," he ordered. "Search pattern."

The four Fokkers separated slightly, each pilot scanning a different sector of sky. Luukkanen's eyes ached from the strain of looking. Where were they?

Then he spotted movement far to the south, two aircraft disappearing into the clouds over Uuraa.

"Contact!" he called. "Two aircraft, to the south. They just entered a cloud."

He banked hard, pushing the Fokker to full throttle, climbing toward the spot where he'd seen the aircraft vanish. The rest of the flight followed, straining to catch up.

They burst through the cloud layer into brilliant sunshine at five thousand feet. The sky was empty in all directions. Luukkanen swore under his breath. They'd lost them.

"Split up," he ordered over the radio. "Vic, you come with me. We'll search south. Tatu, take Illu and sweep east."

"Understood," came Tatu's calm reply.

Luukkanen banked his Fokker toward the coast, descending below the scattered clouds again. For twenty minutes, they saw nothing but the frozen landscape below. His frustration mounted with each passing minute. The enemy had been here. They'd bombed Viipuri, but now they'd vanished.

Then Vic's voice crackled in his headphones. "Two o'clock low! Bomber!"

Luukkanen snapped his head to the right. There, just skimming the treetops, was the unmistakable silhouette of a Tupolev SB-2 bomber. The twin-engined aircraft was heading southeast, making for the border.

Without hesitation, Luukkanen pushed his stick forward and banked right. "I see him. Follow me in."

The Fokker accelerated in the shallow dive, closing rapidly on the unsuspecting bomber. Luukkanen's heart hammered in his chest, but his hands were steady on the controls. Years of training took over. He aligned the Fokker's nose just ahead of the bomber, leading it slightly to compensate for its speed and direction.

At four hundred yards, the SB-2's dorsal gunner spotted them. A stream of tracers arced through the sky toward Luukkanen's Fokker, but the distance was too great for accuracy.

"Steady," Luukkanen murmured to himself, ignoring the incoming fire. Three hundred yards. Two hundred. The bomber grew in his gunsight, its olive-green fuselage and red star markings clearly visible now.

The bomber jinked left, its pilot taking evasive action. Luukkanen adjusted instinctively, keeping his sights on the target. The dorsal gunner was firing continuously now, orange tracers streaking past his cockpit. *One hundred yards.*

Luukkanen's thumb depressed the firing button on top of the control stick. The four 7.62mm machine guns hammered, their vibration shaking the entire aircraft. The sound was deafening even through his helmet. The vicious, ripping thunder of the machineguns firing obliterated the engine noise.

Tracers stitched a line toward the bomber, and Luukkanen saw impacts sparking along its fuselage. The SB-2 lurched but kept flying, its pilot dove to escape him. Luukkanen followed, closing to seventy-five yards. He fired again, a sustained burst that walked from the bomber's left engine across its fuselage.

The Russian aircraft shuddered violently. Smoke began streaming from its left engine nacelle. The dorsal gunner's fire stopped abruptly.

Still, the bomber flew on, now barely fifty feet above

the snow-covered forest. Luukkanen pushed closer, ignoring the risk of collision, determined not to let his quarry escape. Fifty yards now. He could see rivets in the bomber's skin, the determined set of its pilot's shoulders visible through the cockpit glazing.

One more burst. Luukkanen aimed for the right engine and squeezed the trigger. His tracers converged on the engine cowling, punching through metal. Oil sprayed from ruptured lines, black against the gray sky. Flames licked along the nacelle.

The SB-2 banked hard right, trailing smoke and fire. Its nose dropped, but the pilot somehow managed to level out just above the trees. For a moment, Luukkanen thought the aircraft might recover. Then something tore loose from the damaged engine, a piece of cowling or perhaps a propeller blade. The bomber nosed down sharply, clipped the tops of some tall pines, and plowed into a small clearing.

The impact was tremendous. Momentum carried the bomber across the snow, breaking it apart. The cockpit separated from the fuselage, and the wings were sheared off. The wreckage finally came to rest at the edge of the clearing.

Luukkanen circled low, his heart pounding. He'd done it. He'd shot down an enemy bomber. The feeling was indescribable elation mixed with a strange solemnity. Below him lay the shattered remains of a sophisticated machine and, somewhere in that twisted metal, three men.

His radio crackled to life. "Nice shooting!" Vic called; his voice tight with excitement. "Direct hit on both engines!"

Luukkanen banked around for another look at the

crash site. Smoke was rising from the wreckage, but there was no sign of fire. He checked his fuel gauge, still half full, and made a quick mental note of their position.

"I'm going to mark this location," he said to Vic. "Check for landmarks."

They were close to a small village, Koljola, according to his map. There was a railway station visible about two kilometers to the west of the crash site. Luukkanen memorized the location, then made a final pass over the downed bomber.

Three figures were moving away from the wreckage, their dark uniforms stark against the snow. The crew had survived. Luukkanen made a low pass over the railway station, waggling his wings to attract attention, then pointed back toward the crash site. The station personnel, alerted by the sound of the crash, were already rushing out onto the platform.

With a final circle of the area, Luukkanen pulled up and set course back to Immola, Vic tight on his wing. The initial surge of adrenaline was fading, leaving him feeling oddly hollow. He had just killed an aircraft and perhaps its crew, if the local militia or troops found them before they could surrender.

For an hour, they patrolled south of Viipuri, seeing nothing but a few Finnish Bulldogs on a similar mission. Their fuel gauges began to drop toward the red line. It was time to head back.

"Form up," Luukkanen ordered. "We're going home."

As they approached Immola, Luukkanen felt a complex mixture of emotions. Relief at having survived. Pride in his victory. Concern for his missing comrades and a newfound clarity. He had crossed a threshold from which there was no return.

The landing at Immola was automatic. He completed the entire process without consciously thinking about it. Luukkanen taxied to the revetment and shut down the engine. The sudden silence was deafening. He sat for a moment, still strapped in, feeling the adrenaline drain away, leaving a strange calm in its wake.

"Any luck?" Raunio asked as Luukkanen climbed down.

"One SB-2, near Koljola," Luukkanen replied, his voice steadier than he expected. "Direct hits on both engines."

Raunio's face broke into a grin. "Congratulations, sir! First kill of the war for the squadron!"

Luukkanen nodded, suddenly too tired for words. He handed his helmet and gloves to the mechanic, then walked stiffly toward the operations building. His legs felt rubbery, and his back ached from the tension he'd been holding in his muscles.

Magnusson was waiting for them in the operations room. "Report?"

"One enemy bomber shot down, sir," Luukkanen said formally. "A Tupolev SB-2. Crashed near Koljola railway station. Crew survived the crash."

The squadron commander nodded, a slight smile softening his stern features. "Well done, Lieutenant. First confirmed kill of the war."

The phrase hit Luukkanen with unexpected force. *First kill of the war. There would be more, many more. This was just the beginning.*

"And the others?" he asked.

"Tatu and Illu encountered no enemy aircraft. They returned safely half an hour ago." Magnusson's expression grew serious. "Get some food. Your flight is on standby alert until 1500 hours."

"Yes, sir."

The meal in the officers' mess was subdued. No one spoke much. Outside, snow began to fall heavily, reducing visibility to a few hundred yards. Flying would be impossible until it cleared. In a way, Luukkanen was grateful for the respite. It gave him time to process the morning's events, to prepare himself for the next encounter. Because there would be a next encounter. Of that, he was certain.

The snowstorm continued through the night and into the next day, grounding all aircraft. Luukkanen used the time to study intelligence reports on Soviet aircraft types and tactics. The bombers they were likely to encounter were Tupolev SB-2s, twin-engine, three-crew monoplanes with a top speed of 255 mph. Faster than the Fokker's 210 mph in level flight, which meant interception would be challenging.

But now he knew their weakness: the unprotected fuel tanks in the wings, just behind the engines. A well-placed burst there would bring down an SB-2 much more efficiently than peppering its fuselage.

The morning of December 1st dawned clear and cold. The snowfall had stopped, but it had left three feet of fresh powder on the airfield. Ground crews worked frantically to clear a runway while mechanics converted the Fokkers' wheel undercarriages to skis.

By mid-morning, Luukkanen's flight was operational

again. They took off for a patrol over the Gulf of Finland, watching for any sign of renewed Soviet air activity. But the skies remained empty. It seemed the Russians were also taking advantage of the weather respite.

That afternoon, driven by curiosity, Luukkanen borrowed a staff car and drove to Koljola, where he had shot down the SB-2 the previous day. He wanted to examine the wreckage, to see firsthand the effects of his gunfire, to learn how to be more efficient in future engagements.

The small village was blanketed in snow. It was a peaceful and quiet place of tranquility. Occasional military vehicles now interrupted that peacefulness. Luukkanen stopped at the railway station and inquired if anyone had seen the downed aircraft.

"Oh yes," the stationmaster replied eagerly. "It's still there, in Niemi's field, just two kilometers east. They're guarding it."

"And the crew?" Luukkanen asked.

The stationmaster's expression darkened. "Dead. All three. When our men approached to take them prisoner, they opened fire. There was a fight." He shrugged. "What can you do?"

Luukkanen got directions and drove to the site. The bomber was still there, its dark green fuselage stark against the bright whiteness of the snow. The tail had broken off on impact, and one wing was crumpled. But it was remarkably intact for an aircraft that had crashed at speed. A testament to the sturdiness of Soviet engineering.

Pulling up beside the wreck, Luukkanen climbed out of the car, his breath fogging in the cold air. Bullet holes riddled the bomber. He counted over a hundred in the fuselage alone. His marksmanship had been less precise than he'd thought in the heat of combat.

A group of Finnish soldiers stood guard around the wreckage. Their lieutenant approached as Luukkanen examined the aircraft.

"Pilot?" the lieutenant asked, noting Luukkanen's uniform.

"Yes." Luukkanen extended his hand. "Lieutenant Luukkanen, Fighter Squadron 24."

"Lieutenant Järvinen, 5th Infantry." They shook hands. "Your handiwork?"

Luukkanen nodded. "Yesterday morning. My first kill."

"Well done." Järvinen gestured at the bullet holes. "Though you didn't make it easy on yourself. The crew compartment is armored. See how the bullets just punch little dents in the plating?"

Luukkanen examined the area the lieutenant indicated. It was true, many of his rounds had simply bounced off the armor protecting the crew.

"But here," Järvinen continued, pointing to the shattered engine nacelles, "and here," he indicated the wing roots, "no protection at all. That's where you got them. Your fire completely tore apart the left engine. The right one lasted longer but seized up just before they crashed."

Luukkanen walked around the bomber, studying it with professional interest. The manufacturer's plate in the cockpit indicated that the new aircraft had been completed earlier that year. The armor plating around the crew compartment was substantial, explaining why it had taken so many hits to bring it down, but the fuel tanks in the wings were indeed unprotected. A well-placed burst there would bring down an SB-2 much more efficiently than peppering its fuselage.

He filed the information away for future reference. "The crew," he said quietly. "What happened exactly?"

Järvinen's face hardened. "They never intended to surrender. The major, pilot, I think, drew his pistol as soon as our patrol approached. Killed one of my men. The others opened up too. It was over quickly."

Luukkanen nodded, feeling a complicated mix of emotions. He felt relief that he hadn't had to watch their deaths and Sadness for the Finnish soldier who had been killed. A strange respect for the Russian airmen who had fought to the end.

"Thank you for letting me examine the site," he said, shaking Järvinen's hand again. "It's valuable intelligence."

The drive back to Immola gave Luukkanen time to think. How strange that three men he had never met, whose faces he had never seen, were now dead because of his actions. Yet he felt no guilt. They had bombed Viipuri. They had killed Finnish civilians. And if they had escaped, they would have been back the next day to kill more.

This was war. It was not personal or murder. It was not even hate, just simply duty.

When he reached the base, the news of his victory had spread. Pilots from other squadrons stopped by to offer congratulations. Even Colonel Lorentz made an appearance, shaking Luukkanen's hand with uncharacteristic warmth.

In the officers' mess that night, someone produced a

bottle of cognac. Toasts were made and backs were slapped. People asked questions about the engagement. Questions Luukkanen answered as best he could, though the reality of combat proved both more vivid and more fragmentary than anyone expected.

As the celebration wound down and the officers drifted back to their quarters, Luukkanen found himself sitting alone by the stove, nursing the last of his drink. The initial elation had faded, replaced by a more complex emotion he couldn't immediately identify.

Pride, yes. He had done what he was trained to do. He had defended his country, destroyed an enemy bomber that might otherwise have killed Finnish civilians.

There was something else, too that went with it. A sobriety. It was almost as if an invisible weight had been added to his shoulders. Three men had died by his hand. Men whose faces he had never seen, whose names he would never know. Men who, like him, had been following orders, flying a mission for their country.

Captain Magnusson appeared in the doorway, watching him with understanding. "First one's always the strangest," he whispered, crossing to sit opposite Luukkanen. "You don't know whether to celebrate or mourn."

Luukkanen nodded, grateful that someone understood. "I keep thinking about them. The crew."

"That's natural." Magnusson's face was serious in the dim light. "But remember why we're fighting. Those bastards crossed our border and bombed our cities. That greedy bastard in Moscow started this war, not us."

"I know." Luukkanen stared into his glass. "I don't regret it. I'd do it again in a heartbeat. It's just. . ."

"Different than you expected," Magnusson finished for him. "War always is. But remember what I said yesterday. You're a real fighter pilot now. You've faced the enemy and lived to tell about it."

Luukkanen considered this, then nodded slowly. "Yes, I suppose I have."

The captain clapped him on the shoulder. "Get some sleep. The Russians will be back tomorrow, and the next day, and the day after that. This was just the beginning."

Later, lying in his bunk, Luukkanen replayed the engagement in his mind, analyzing his performance, noting mistakes, planning improvements. How to conserve ammunition. When to break off pursuit. The ideal attack angle to hit those vulnerable engine nacelles and fuel tanks.

What stayed with him most vividly was not the technical aspects of the fight, but the surge of clarity he had felt in those crucial moments. The absolute focus and certainty of purpose he felt coupled with the knowledge that he was exactly where he was meant to be, doing exactly what he was trained to do. He had become a combat pilot. Finland's first aerial victor in this new war.

Outside, snow began to fall again, covering Immola airfield in a fresh blanket of white. The wind carried the distant rumble of artillery from the border. Tomorrow would bring new missions, new challenges, perhaps new victories or defeats.

But for now, Lieutenant Eino Luukkanen closed his eyes, letting exhaustion claim him at last. In his dreams, he flew his Fokker through clear blue skies, hunting for the enemy, defending Finland with newly proven skill and determination.

The first blood had been drawn. There would be more

before this war was done.

Other Books By James Mullins

The Winter Sniper

The world has frozen into a battlefield, and the blood of the brave stains the snow.

One young sniper dares to defy the largest army on earth. Will Hale Karhonen survive the Winter War, or will he become another forgotten body buried beneath the endless white?

Join the fight today and experience a story of resilience, heartbreak, and unyielding courage.

Special Military Operation

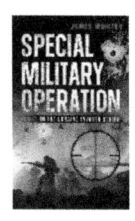

Two Men. One War. No Second Chances.
One's a broken Soviet sniper. The other, a rejected youth with something to prove.

When Russia invades Ukraine, Andrei Kuznetsov emerges from exile, gripping his grandfather's battered rifle. By his side stands Sasha—young, untested, and desperate for redemption.

Together, they'll face bullets, betrayal, and their own inner demons.

Read the gripping military thriller where redemption meets resistance. Get your copy now and join the fight.

Afterword

Thus far my writing has focused on the plight of individual soldiers as they battle overwhelming odds in the defense of their homeland. I wanted to try something different that pulled on my own military experiences in the Air Force. Since so many readers like you have enjoyed The Winter Sniper series, I decided that my first attempt at an aviation fiction novel would be during the Winter War! Thus the Wings Of The Winter War series was born. I hope you enjoyed the stories and will see you back for Book II in the series for Veikko's and Eino's next mission.

If you'd like to drop me a direct line, I'd love to hear what you think about the story, or whatever else is on your mind. Feedback is greatly appreciated. You can email me directly at jamesmullinsauthor@yahoo.com

Thanks for reading!

About the Author

James Mullins is the author of sixteen novels, including *Wolfpack Leader*, drawing from a lifelong passion for history and a diverse background. He holds a Master's and Bachelor's degree in Business Administration, as well as an Associate's degree in Acquisition and Contract Management.
James served in the United States Air Force as an Avionics Attack Systems Specialist with the 71st Fighter Squadron, the Ironmen, completing deployments in both the Middle East and Iceland. These experiences fostered a deep respect for resilience in extreme environments, an element often reflected in his writing.
After his military service, James managed the Pest Control Department for Patriot Pest Control,

where he humorously claims to have "slain millions of bugs for the betterment of humankind." He later joined Newport News Shipbuilding, where for thirteen years he supported the construction of Nimitz- and Ford-class aircraft carriers and Virginia-class submarines. His roles included supply chain management, forecasting methodologies, and overhaul production control. In his final year there, he applied his writing skills to successfully navigate federal audits.

Today, James works as the Finance Manager for Virginia with the U.S. Department of Transportation's Federal Highway Administration, helping the Virginia Department of Transportation access and apply federal highway funds to maintain and expand its transportation network.

James lives in Virginia with his brilliantly supportive wife Anna, their sons Tristan and Parker. His love of history, particularly ancient Rome, Byzantium, the Middle Ages, World War II, and the American Civil War, continues to inspire the stories he brings to life.

Printed in Dunstable, United Kingdom